Fields of GOLD

TARNISHED SOULS

Fields
of
GOLD

TARNISHED SOULS

DEV BENTHAM

www.DevBentham.com

Tarnished Souls 2: Fields of Gold
Copyright © September 2012 by Dev Bentham

ISBN 978-1-942255-00-0
Cover Artist: Jordan Castillo Price
This story was previously published by Loose Id LLC.
Larke Butler edited the first edition.

Printed in the United States of America

Published by
Love is a Light Press
POB 685, Minocqua, WI 54548

Dedication

For Jer,
I swear in the days still left…

Acknowledgments

I can't begin to thank Jordan Castillo Price enough for reading this story in its infancy, offering incredible insights on how to grow it up and then creating this BEAUTIFUL cover. I am also deeply indebted to my wonderful Loose Id editor, Larke Butler, who helped immensely with the first edition of this book. And thanks (!) to Laurie Cheeley for lending me her wonderful copyediting skills.

This is the second in my Loose Id series of Jewish holiday stories. If you read the Passover story, Learning from Isaac, *you'll recognize Nathan and Isaac, who show up in this book as secondary characters. This story centers around Rosh Hashanah, the Jewish New Year, and by implication, Yom Kippur, the Day of Atonement. Together these constitute the High Holidays, a time for reflection, reconsideration, and the making of amends.*

Being human is a messy business. And real love means saying you're sorry. Often.

Chapter One

Market booths lined the eight blocks around the Capitol Square. They faced the dense throng of shoppers pushing strollers, walking dogs and trudging the sidewalk looking for plants, produce, baked goods, free-range meats, artisan-crafted cheeses, jewelry and soap. Traffic inched along outside, pausing for pedestrians who emerged at random from between booths to stroll across the street in search of cash, coffee or their cars. Even the bike lane felt crowded. I slowed to let a swarm of spandex-clad enthusiasts fly by and stopped to wait for a bus to pull out.

It took a few minutes before I could slide back into the stream, but as I headed down the hill, I picked up speed. I rounded the corner where abortion activists warred with green-shirted environmentalists for space. Half a block down, my attention was caught by a sudden flash of very white teeth and blond curls. When I looked back at the road, a man carrying two bushy tomato plants stepped out from between two cars. I swerved to miss him. A car horn blared, and I got a glimpse of a giant black SUV bearing down on me from the outside lane just before it grazed my back tire, throwing me out of control. My bike bounced over the curb and into a tree. I went nose over handlebars and tumbled through the crowd to land at the gorgeous, smiling man's feet. The fall hurt, and not just my pride.

"Oh my God, are you okay?" His eyes were wide and the loveliest shade of blue. He'd dropped to his knees beside me, and I would have liked to make a joke about going down and knees, except all I could do was hold my ankle and try not to moan. Other faces peered down at me. A woman shouldered her way through the crowd, muttering something about being a doctor.

"I'm fine." I dropped my leg and tried to sit up. Pain spiked through me, and I almost lost my breakfast, which would have completed my humiliation.

The woman pushed me back down. "I'm Dr. Goldstein. Relax. Let me take a look. Pete, see what you can do to make him comfortable."

Pete must have been the man beside me with the wonderful smile because he slid a wadded-up jacket under my head. I gritted my teeth and tried not to cry out as she pulled off my shoe, poked, and prodded. Staring up at the gathering of Saturday morning shoppers, I prayed for someone to say, "Move along. Nothing to see here."

Pete raised his voice. "Logan, haul his bike over to the stall. It's blocking traffic." He beamed those beautiful teeth at the crowd. "Thanks, everyone. I think we've got it here."

People nodded, murmured, gaped a little more, and shuffled off.

"Thanks," I managed to get out before Dr. Goldstein gave my ankle a particularly painful twist and I almost blacked out.

Pete looked down at me. Dazzling, that smile— almost enough to let me forget the pain.

I held his gaze. He held mine.

His smile widened. "No problem. It's been a while since I had a guy fall at my feet like that."

Dr. Goldstein snorted and took my arm. "Let's get you up and see if that ankle can hold any weight."

Pete grabbed my other arm, and between them they managed to get me to my feet. My ankle hurt, but it held, and Pete's hand on my arm was pleasantly distracting. They steered me over to a chair by Pete's booth. Dr. Goldstein squatted and propped my naked foot on an upside-down five-gallon bucket. She turned to Pete. "Do you have any ice?"

"Sure." He started scooping ice from a cooler into a plastic produce bag.

When it was about half-full, Dr. Goldstein draped it over my ankle and gave me a firm, motherly look. "It appears to be a bad sprain. My guess is at least second, if not third degree. What's your insurance situation?"

I frowned. "Two-hundred-dollar deductible, ten percent after that. I don't really have two hundred dollars. I'd rather not get the medical profession involved, no offense."

She stood, brushing off her slacks. "None taken. While I'm all for Obamacare, I'd prefer we'd adopted the Canadian system. I doubt anything's broken, but of course, I can't be certain without an X-ray. You'll want to wrap your foot, ice that ankle for fifteen minutes several times a day, keep off it, and elevate it for the next few days. Try not to let it stiffen up. Writing the alphabet with your toes is one common exercise for sprained ankles. If the swelling doesn't go down and it's still too painful to get around on, you'll have to come in." She handed me her business card. "Call my office. That will be cheaper than an emergency room visit."

I stared at the business card in my hand. Dr. Stella Goldstein. "Thanks. That's really nice of you."

Dr. Goldstein glanced at Pete. "No problem. Jakobsen's has the best produce in the market. Any friend of theirs is a friend of mine."

With a grin, Pete held out a large carton of raspberries. "On the house. Thanks, Doc."

She took the berries and held them close to her nose. "These smell absolutely wonderful. And they're gorgeous—so red. Thank you." She nodded toward me. "Get that ankle taped, and don't let him move around too much."

Pete actually winked at me as he assured her that I wasn't going anywhere soon. *Ooh, sassy.* After she wandered away, Pete called over the scrawny, dark-haired middle schooler who was leaning my twisted bike against the back of the produce booth.

Pete pulled a wallet out of his jeans pocket. "Logan, I need you to run over to the drugstore and get an elastic bandage."

The only reason I'd braved the Saturday market traffic in the first place was to get to the bank in time to transfer the last of my savings to cover a check I'd already sent, the one that would pay my cell phone bill through the summer. At least I'd managed to get the deposit in before the accident. It would be another three months before I got a paycheck. I had a roof over my head, a phone, and not much else. But appearances to the contrary, I had my pride. I struggled onto one hip, reaching for my own back pocket. "You don't have to pay for that."

Pete settled a hand on my shoulder and pushed me back down. "You can pay me back later. You got a name?"

His hand felt warm and strong. I turned toward him and noticed the golden hair covering his deeply tanned forearm. I tried to smile up at him, but my ankle really hurt and my expression probably looked more like a grimace. I cleared my throat. "Avi Rosen."

He nodded, his hand still gentle on my shoulder. He smelled like sunshine and green plants. "Pete Jakobsen. And that little whip-poor-will is my nephew, Logan, who's about to get us all a lemonade on his way back from the drugstore." He handed his nephew a bill. Logan sprinted in the direction of State Street.

A large woman pushing a baby stroller pulled up to the produce booth, and I looked at Pete's wares for the first time. Rows of cardboard containers stamped JAKOBSEN in bold letters, filled with peas, potatoes, zucchini, blueberries, blackberries and raspberries covered one side of the table. Turnips were mounded between a stack of rhubarb stalks and several huge bins overflowing with various kinds of lettuces. Buckets of flower bouquets sat on the ground in front of the booth.

I watched Pete interacting with his customer, feeling my heart rate slow and that shaky, shocky feeling dissipate. Broad-shouldered and muscular, he towered over the mother as she pointed to containers, which he settled gently on the scale, all the time keeping up a laughing banter that had her batting her eyelashes at him. I couldn't help thinking of the feel of his hand on my shoulder. *Dream on, honey. This one plays for my team.*

Despite the pain in my ankle, it was pleasant sitting beside the booth, watching Pete weigh produce and make change. The fair exchange of goods seemed pure. I felt that way about teaching—that it was a clean trading of ideas. Research, on the other hand, was more about untangling moldy string— the bits often fell apart in my fingers. What did it mean that I was a little relieved to be grounded in this sunny place for the morning, unable to get to the library and whack away again at the notes for my long overdue dissertation?

The crowd inched by in a perpetual circle around the Capitol, and by the time Logan reappeared with beverages and bandage, Pete had sold a few dozen bags of food. Logan pressed a red-and-white paper cup, sweaty with condensation, into my hand. I took a long refreshing gulp.

"Thanks, kid." Pete accepted his cup and patted Logan's back. "Take over the booth, will ya, while I wrap our patient's foot."

"You don't have to do that." I leaned forward, reaching for the packaged bandage.

Pete held it out of my reach, like a big kid playing keep-away. I stopped flailing around and tried to regain my dignity. "You have a thing for rescuing people or something?"

He set his drink on the ground, squatted in front of my bucket-propped foot, and slid off the melted ice pack. "Beats having you sue me. You wouldn't believe what my liability insurance rates are, and that's without any claims."

I stared at him. "Sue you?"

The firm hand he ran along my calf, pushing up my jeans, sent a shiver up my leg. "This is the capitol. Everyone's a lawyer. You can't be too careful." He looked up at me from under pale gold lashes. I've always been a sucker for freckles. The bandage wrapping crackled. I blinked and refocused on what he was saying, which turned out to be just as enticing. "Besides, I was staring at you and picturing how good you'd look in racer spandex. Who knows, maybe you were looking at me instead of paying attention to the road." He fluttered his eyelids at me. "I can always hope."

I winced as he pulled a loop of bandage tight around my throbbing ankle. "Are you always such a flirt?"

He secured the bandage end and patted my knee. "Only around pretty boys who need distraction. How does that feel?"

I wiggled my toes experimentally, sending sharp twinges up my calf. I had to admit the damned thing felt better wrapped up. "Thanks." I considered my mangled bicycle. "Can I leave that here for a while? I'll catch the bus and get someone to help me pick it up later."

Pete put his hands on his thighs and pressed himself up. "No way. Doc Stella buys at least twenty dollars of produce from me every week. If she says you need to stay off your feet, that's exactly what you're going to do. I can't afford to piss her off." He looked at his watch. "We've got a few more hours until closing. I'll drive you home then." His gaze settled on mine. "You got someone to make you chicken soup once you're there?"

I blinked, trying to picture Jack making soup. Not that it mattered. With the legislature not in session, Jack wasn't around much. He'd be up in Eagle River, and Mrs. Jack would be making the soup. But not for me. I cleared my throat. "There's always takeout."

He flipped open his phone. "Hi, Sis. You know that old set of crutches? Can you bring those when you come? I think they're in the barn." He paused and glanced toward the booth. "No, he's fine. A friend sprained his ankle." He laughed and rolled his eyes. "None of your business. Just bring the crutches, okay?" Snapping the phone shut, he smiled at me. "We need to make sure you can get to the door when the pizza man comes."

"Uncle Pete?" Logan gestured toward the line forming in front of the booth. He sounded impatient.

"Coming." Pete held up his hand like he was staying a dog. "Don't move."

I eyed my pack full of photocopied articles. As pleasant as it was to sit in the sun, there really was no excuse for avoiding my research. I nodded. "I'll stay put, but would you please toss me my bag? I've got reading to do."

Or pretend to do. The morning wore on, and I found myself distracted from the dry nineteenth-century prose of the paper I was trying to read. Debates in the 1787 New York Convention about adoption of the Federal Constitution couldn't compete with the sights, sounds and smells of a very present, crowded farmers' market. And like with anything else, the insider experience, in this case the event from behind the booth, was totally different, and I found it completely engrossing. Customers traded recipes with Pete, talked with Logan about school and commented on the vegetables, asked when tomatoes would be in season, discussed the weather, and gossiped about other booths. My ankle got another icing, and with gritted teeth, I tried to write the alphabet with my toes. Only got to *E*. Toward the end of the morning, other vendors began showing up, trading a loaf of bread, a pie, some cinnamon rolls or a slab of cheese for peas, potatoes and berries.

A tall, red-faced man stopped to buy three large bundles of flowers. He and Pete chatted for a few minutes about weather predictions for the next week.

As he walked away, Pete shook his head. "I'm betting the flowers won't be enough to win her forgiveness."

I stared after the man, who was pressing his way through the crowd. "Do you know him?"

He shrugged. "It's late Saturday morning. He still smells like booze, and he's buying an armload of flowers. She's probably home crying or packing."

"And you got all that from a two-minute encounter?" Home, crying or packing—because that's what wronged wives did, right? I tried to ignore the twinge of guilt that came with that particular image.

Pete reached under the booth and brought out the bakery sack of cheese empanadas he'd procured in exchange for veggies. He handed one to Logan, one to me, and bit into a third. "You'd be surprised how much you can get from first impressions." He leaned a hip against his produce table and contemplated me. "For example, you're a student at the university. Given what you said about insurance, you're probably a graduate teaching or research assistant. History?"

I fluffed the sheaf of papers in my lap. "Elementary, my dear Sherlock."

Pete laughed and stuffed the rest of the empanada into his mouth. When he could talk again, he held my gaze. "There isn't anyone you'd call for chicken soup, but somehow I don't think that's the whole story."

I looked away, the fun suddenly out of the game. I gestured toward the sidewalk where a woman fingered a basket of peas while Logan weighed potatoes for an older man in a jogging suit. "You've got a customer."

Pete arched one eyebrow and moved to help the woman. When he turned back to me, I made sure my nose was buried in eighteenth-century politics.

Chapter Two

As the crowd thinned, customers began striking bargains for the remaining produce. By early afternoon, the only things left on his table were a few bags of lettuce, several stalks of rhubarb, and three baskets of potatoes. These got tossed into a cardboard box before Logan and Pete started disassembling the booth. The ambient noise shifted as the shuffling of the crowd gave way to the banging and slamming of other vendors doing the same.

Shortly after two, a battered blue pickup pulled up to the curb. Pete's sister, Brynne, turned out to be a shorter, slimmer version of her brother. I guessed both to be in their mid-thirties but had no idea who was older. They had the tanned skin of people who spent time outdoors, blond hair that would only get lighter as the summer progressed, and a casual jokey way with each other that looked like love. Logan had let me know he'd recently finished fourth grade, and no one mentioned his dad.

Brynne strode toward me, fiddling with the butterfly bolts on a pair of battered wooden crutches. "Pete used these last. Looks like we need to shorten them by a few inches."

I struggled to stand and took one step. My ankle was enormous and hurt like hell, but at least it held my weight. I gratefully accepted the crutches. "This is very nice of you. I'll bring them back, I promise."

She cocked her head and considered me. "At least you're not a puppy. His last rescue took months to housetrain."

"Getting Homer to go outside did not take months," Logan called. "You always exaggerate."

Torn between asking about Homer, assuring Brynne I wouldn't pee on the floor, and blowing off the whole rescue thing, I missed the opportunity for a retort altogether. Brynne turned away and began gathering folding chairs.

Pete gave me another of his winks as he passed near, carrying the front half of the folded table that had recently groaned with vegetables. Logan trailed behind, his face set as he concentrated on keeping his edge of the table from scraping the sidewalk. I stood watching, completely useless as they efficiently folded the booth into the back of the truck.

"Where do you live?" Pete asked as he threw my mangled bike on top of the pile and slammed the tailgate shut.

"Close, on Willie Street." I lifted one crutch and pointed in a vaguely eastward direction, painfully aware that I could have walked the distance if I had two functional feet.

Brynne put an arm around Logan and pointed down the block. "We'll go help Barbara load her plants. Roger's mom's sick, and she's all alone this week. Drop off your rescued Fay Wray and come back to get us." Did I look that helpless? But she said it in such a friendly tone that I couldn't feel insulted.

"We're here every Wednesday and Saturday," she continued with a smirk as she patted Logan on the back to move him in the direction of the tomato plants. "Or maybe Pete will give you his card."

I turned to Pete, who was busy tying down his load. "Is she always that forthright?"

He shook his head, a smile playing around the edges of his mouth, and looked at me across the truck bed. "Yes." He jerked the rope tight and patted the truck. It rang with a hollow metal drum sound. "That about does it. Hop in and I'll drive you home."

I swung into motion with bad leg bent and my messenger bag banging my ass. There's an odd swooping grace to walking on crutches that took me a moment to find. By the time I rounded the truck, I felt almost in control of my mobility. Pete opened the door and held the crutches as I hoisted my ass onto the seat. One look at his biceps told me he could probably pick me up and toss me in, but he let me struggle on my own, for which I was profoundly grateful. My pride had taken enough of a battering without him playing King Kong to my Fay Wray.

The inside of the truck smelled of manure, old vinyl and diesel. Pete slammed the door shut, hit the clutch, turned the key, and eventually the engine roared to life. I fidgeted in the seat, trying to find a comfortable position for my foot.

Pete shifted the truck into gear. We eased into traffic before he spoke. "Are you involved with anyone?"

The question shouldn't have caught me off guard. We'd been flirting around it all morning. Still, I found myself stammering. "Uh, sort of. I mean, yes, but we're not exclusive."

He glanced at me. "Not exclusive. An open relationship, or you haven't decided if you like each other?"

"It's complicated."

"Uh-huh." Pete signaled and turned off the square, heading down Willie Street.

I pointed to a tall apartment building, visible in the distance. "That's it, on the right."

"Not exactly student digs." He gestured toward the lakefront. "Nice view?"

I shifted again in my seat. "Um, yeah. But we face the Capitol."

"You and Mr. Not-Exclusive?" I could feel myself blushing under his gaze.

"Um, well, I caretake the place, actually." Crap, there was a reason I didn't talk with anyone about my private life. No one except my friend Isaac, who I knew would understand. "Drop me by the front entrance. I can take it from there."

Pete turned into the parking lot and stopped. He stared out at Lake Monona, drumming his fingers on the steering wheel.

I twisted to grab the crutches from behind the bench seat. "Hey, thanks for everything. You've been great. I'll get these back to you as soon as I can." I was babbling but couldn't stop myself. I popped open the truck's door.

The sound seemed to wake Pete. "Wait."

He opened his own door and trotted around the back of the truck. Oh great, just what I needed, to be helped out of the truck by my very own Good Samaritan.

"Really, I'm fine." I slid from the seat, wincing as my foot hit the door on the way out.

He slung my battered bike out of the truck and gestured toward the building. "You want me to take this in for you?"

I contemplated my wounded warhorse. The handlebars jutted to the side at an odd angle, the front wheel bent almost double, and one foot pedal was twisted ninety degrees out of plumb. I rummaged in my front pocket for the bike lock key and tossed it to him. "There's a rack behind the building. Although, who would steal it now?"

The trip from the truck to the front door took me almost as long as it took Pete to stow my bike and return. He handed me the key, stepped into the open door, rummaged in his back pocket and pulled out his wallet. He fished out a card and thrust it toward me. "Here."

I took it. His bulk blocked my way. I inhaled that odd combination of fresh plants and diesel. He had a good four inches on me, and I had to tilt my head to look up at him. "Thanks."

He ran a hand through his hair. "Look. It's been a long time since I was anyone's piece on the side, but then"—he gave a dry laugh—"it's been a long time, period. So, well, if you're interested, give me a call. Or if you need help, or that chicken soup, or anything."

His eyes were Independence Day blue. The air between us felt ten degrees warmer than it had a moment before. I tucked his card into my front pocket. "Thanks. I might take you up on that."

He ran a calloused finger lightly along my jaw. "I hope so."

With that, he was striding toward the truck. I watched him go before struggling into the elevator and up to the sixth floor.

* * * *

I tossed a frozen potpie in the microwave and ate it standing at the sink while another heated. My ankle throbbed, but it felt like too much work to maneuver a plate of food to the kitchen table. The floury filling burned my tongue on the first bite, and the middle tasted like cold mush. I choked them both down. Everything seemed to take forever as I filled a bag with ice, grabbed ibuprofen and a beer, and hobbled one-crutched to the couch. By the time I propped pillows behind me and under my foot, settled the ice over my throbbing ankle and popped open the beer, I was exhausted. Out the picture window, the Capitol building thrust into the rich blue sky like an advertisement for democracy. I pulled Pete's card from my pocket. It was one of those generic designs you can get cheap on the Internet—a flat wheat field vista, a basket of tomatoes, peppers and asparagus in the upper left-hand corner. *Jakobsen's Farms* and a Marshall, Wisconsin address were printed in the upper right with the Web address given below. Pete and Brynne Jakobsen's names were in the lower left along with a phone number. A family farm, how fucking wholesome. I rolled a bitter mouthful of pale ale across my tongue.

I'd said I was in an open relationship. Was I? It wasn't like Jack and I had ever talked about monogamy. I hadn't been with anyone else since we got together. But by definition, a relationship with a married man wasn't exclusive, right? Still, picking up the phone to call Pete felt like a betrayal.

As if on cue, my phone rang. I lurched for my bag, out of reach on the coffee table. I was breathless by the time I found the phone and noted the caller ID.

I answered it. "Jack."

"Hi." The tightness of his tone let me know he wasn't alone. "How are you?"

I glanced at my foot. "All right, I guess. How about you?"

"Fine, fine. I'm calling to let you know I'll be there next week. Richardson scheduled a meeting of the subcommittee on farm affairs. I'm driving down tomorrow night."

I tried not to sigh. I had hoped he wouldn't be in town for another week. I waited to speak until I could be sure I sounded enthusiastic. "Good."

I watched a pigeon settle on the windowsill while I waited for him to continue.

He cleared his throat. "Yes, well, I wanted to make sure you had the place ready for me. I know how you college students are."

"It will be nice to see you." Early in our relationship, back when it had felt like a relationship, I'd enjoyed torturing him with suggestive comments during our multileveled conversations. He never responded well, though, and it had started to feel hollow.

More throat clearing. "Yes, well. See you then." The line clicked dead.

I leaned back on the couch, closed my eyes, and pictured Jack slipping his phone into the breast pocket of his suit. Or setting it on the kitchen table and turning back to a game with his sons. Or enfolding his wife in his arms. I shook my head. That kind of thinking didn't help. I gave Pete's card one more glance, then stuffed it regretfully back into my jeans pocket.

Chapter Three

It took about four hours to drive from Eagle River to Madison. Jack liked to have dinner with the family before leaving home. I worked on The Project, as I'd taken to calling my dissertation, until ten, after which I bundled my pile of note cards and papers into my bag and slid it into place on the lowest bookshelf. I lowered the blinds on all the windows, ensuring no one would see the assemblyman when he arrived. Everything took longer than I expected. I was out of the shower and had finished re-taping my ankle when I heard his key in the lock. Wrapped in the silky blue robe Jack bought me for Christmas, I grabbed the crutches and swung out of the bathroom.

I'd met Jack when a budget cut in the history department left me without a teaching assistantship for the fall semester, and I had taken a job giving tours of the Capitol building to out-of-state tourists and school field trips. We passed in the halls and nodded in greeting to each other in the cafeteria. That was it until one day Jack embraced gay stereotypes by approaching me in the men's room. He wasn't one of the two out gay men serving in the Wisconsin State Legislature, and since he wasn't from either Madison or Milwaukee, he wouldn't become the third. Evidently Eagle River likes its representatives in reproductive pairs.

It started as a real affair, with me crushed out on how he dressed and walked, his urgent meetings with other lawmakers, firm handshakes with voters, the certainty with which he spoke—all the accoutrements of power. So what if he had a wife and I was a secret? I couldn't afford to get attached anyway, since finding a job after graduation would undoubtedly take me far away from Madison. It seemed a fair trade, especially when he sweetened the deal with free rent. And I cared about him. Not love exactly, but certainly affection.

Jack looked distinguished, even in his weekend duds. He was tall and thin, with wisps of gray at the temples, but mostly it was the way he carried himself, all self-determination and confidence. If capitalism had a mascot, it would be Jack. When we were first together, I got off on that self-assured grace of his, and seeing him in a three-piece suit had made me sweat.

But everything cools over time, doesn't it?

As he walked in the door, he looked flush and carried his briefcase in one hand and a light jacket in the other. He dropped his case on the bench in the entryway and draped his jacket over it. When he turned toward me, he revealed both a giant hard-on pressing out the front of his pants and a pair of fur-lined restraints clutched in his hand.

He leered. "I brought you a present."

My heart sank. I should have seen it coming. He'd been hinting for weeks. Still. I looked from the restraints to Jack's red face. "Um, bondage isn't really my—"

He held a finger to his lips. "Shhh. You'll like it. I promise."

I swallowed and reminded myself that Jack had been really generous with me. I owed him. And I couldn't afford to piss him off right now. It was just sex play, right? I looked into his hungry eyes and nodded.

He gestured to my foot. "What happened to you?"

"Sprained it." I held up the injured ankle.

His brow furrowed. "Does it hurt?"

I flexed my foot gingerly. "Not too much."

"Good." His gaze traveled down my body in a lascivious wave. "It's good to see you."

That look used to be enough to get me rock hard. It could still evoke a little zing. I nodded toward the bulge in his chinos. "I can see that."

He stepped closer, his hand going to the belt of my robe. He tugged and it swung open. He stepped back and looked at me. "You look sexy like that, trapped and available. God, that's hot." He unzipped his pants and produced his dick, already hard from whatever he'd been thinking on the drive down. He stroked it absently. "See what I've got for you?"

I'm a sucker for a hard cock, pun intended, and the sight of his purple head finally sent a surge of energy right to my prick. I'm not good with dirty talk. I always think it sounds stupid coming out of my mouth. I try to make up for it with my eyes, which Jack once called dark pools of sex appeal. I use them as much as I can.

He stepped forward, his fingers sliding through my hair. I dropped the crutches and lurched to my knees. I closed my eyes as pain shot up my leg. His fingers tightened in my hair. It didn't hurt as long as I held my head still.

"Suck my cock, pretty boy."

I slid my lips over the head and my own cock stiffened. I can't help but get excited when someone around me is turned on, really turned on. I once asked my best friend Isaac—who used be a prostitute—how he managed sex when he didn't want the man who was paying. He told me there was always something he could focus on that would get him hot.

I concentrated on the feel of Jack's cock in my hand and the taste of him on my tongue. He pulled out and half dragged me to the bedroom where he threw me on my belly and cuffed my hands high on the bed frame. I had to hold on to the restraints to keep them from pulling my wrists. Even so, the cuffs bit into my flesh. With a quick slap of lube on his condom-clad cock he pushed in, pounding into my ass until I felt raw. I pressed my face into my biceps and ignored the way my ankle throbbed with his every thrust. Jack held my shoulders, riding into me hard and fast. His breathing changed. I could feel him get close.

He grabbed my cock and started pumping in rhythm with the slam of his dick. I cast about for an image to send me over the edge and suddenly saw Pete's mouth, red and full around my cock, and I was tumbling down that familiar rabbit hole, spilling onto the sweat-stained sheets.

* * * *

Jack stood in the bathroom, straightening his tie in the mirror. "I don't know how late I'll be tonight."

"Okay." I lay naked on the bed, watching him get ready.

"I left some cash on the table. We're almost out of coffee. Maybe you could get groceries." He gave the tie one last tug, picked up his briefcase, ruffled my hair and left.

I stared at the ceiling. My ankle and ass both throbbed. I glanced at my wrists where red bracelets of bruises were beginning to purple. What would they have looked like if the cuffs hadn't been lined with fur? I rolled one sore shoulder and the other before levering myself up to sit on the edge of the bed. This new kink of Jack's wouldn't have been my first choice. The only really sexy thing about the whole evening had been seeing Pete's mouth around my cock. And that had been imaginary. Although Pete had been pretty clear it didn't have to be. I shook my head. That thought wasn't something I could indulge right now.

The crutches would be on the living room floor where I'd dropped them before Jack had half carried, half marched me to the bedroom. Pink flesh bulged around the bandage on my ankle. I unwrapped it, trying not to wince as pain bolted through me every time I moved. The swollen outside of my ankle was deep red and dark blue. At least it matched my wrists.

I stood on my good leg and hopped to the kitchen. Ten twenties lay on the kitchen table, still crisp from an ATM. He must have stopped at a cash machine on his way down. There was about half a cup of coffee left in the pot. I poured that, grabbed the ice bag from the freezer, propped my foot on a chair, and tried not to think too hard about my life.

My phone rang from the living room. By the time I got there, it had stopped. I lay down on the living room floor next to my crutches. I fingered the wood, wondering idly about the old barn where they'd been stored. Brynne had said that Pete was the last person who'd used them. I scrunched my jeans into a pillow and called my mother back.

I once heard this story about this guy who calls his mom. She says, "Oy, I haven't eaten in days." He says, "Mom, why aren't you eating," and she says, "In case you called, God forbid I should have my mouth full."

Mom answered on the first ring.

I grew up in Milwaukee, and before you start thinking *That '70s Show*, we lived on the north side in an odd little neighborhood of African Americans and ultra-Orthodox Jews. Until seventh grade I went to school at a yeshiva and sported a buzz cut and *peyes*—those long curls that drip down by the ears—like a shtetl kid from the old country. Mom hated it. Evidently Dad got increasingly more religious after they were married and dragged her into the community, pregnant with me. When I was twelve, my father started talking about marrying off my oldest sister, who was seventeen, and mom blew up. My parents split and Mom moved all five kids farther north. My high school years were spent shuttling back and forth the three miles between late twentieth-century America and nineteenth-century Poland.

Two of my sisters still see my dad. Another won't. My brother lives in Dad's community, peyes and all. At this point, I'm not in contact with my brother or my father. Dad and I had a blowout fight when I came out. He sends me postcards every Rosh Hashanah, inviting me to repent and telling me that he'll find a nice girl for me to marry, one who won't expect too much. For his world, that's a loving response.

Mom's quieter in her disapproval. Madison is a ninety-minute bus ride from Milwaukee, but I only get home for Passover in the spring and the High Holidays—Rosh Hashanah and Yom Kippur—in the fall. She drives over to meet me for lunch every few months, and we talk on the phone.

"Avi, I was in the grocery, and I ran into Danny Gross's mother. Do you remember Danny Gross from high school?"

Who can forget the school bully? "Sure, Mom. I remember him. Didn't he become a banker or something?"

"Stockbroker." Her breath came out in a whoosh. "And the word around the neighborhood is that he's been indicted for securities fraud. Such a *shanda*. Of course, his mother told me he's taking a leave of absence from his job to think things through. Who does she think she's kidding? He'll have plenty of time to think in prison. I never liked him. He was very mean to you."

Sometimes my mother says the perfect thing.

"Security fraud," I responded. "Wow, that's serious."

"He was a hideous boy. He called you terrible names."

I nodded at the ceiling, remembering Danny Gross's pinched face. "He was a schmuck, all right."

"His mother is a piece of work too. She had the gall to ask me if you were still a homosexual." And sometimes she says something perfectly awful.

I closed my eyes. "Did you tell her that yes, I am?"

"I told her no such thing. It's none of her business."

I kept my voice level. "Mama, I'm not going to change. This is me."

She was silent a long time. Eventually she sighed. "I know. But it's not what I wanted for you. How are you? Are you getting enough to eat?"

I opened my eyes and looked down at my naked, aching body. "Sure. I'm getting plenty to eat."

After we hung up, I rewrapped my ankle, pulled on jeans, got my backpack, hobbled to the bus stop, rode to the grocery, and spent one of the twenties on food. By the time I got back to the apartment and put away the coffee, cream, eggs, and bread, I was exhausted, but I pulled out The Project, determined to make some intellectual headway.

I was still working—sitting up in bed, trying to outline my damned introduction—when Jack got home. He brushed his teeth, changed into his favorite plaid pajamas, and climbed in beside me.

I piled my papers on the bedside table, glad for the excuse to put them down, and turned out the light. "I have an early meeting with my adviser tomorrow morning."

"What does she want?" Jack's not a cuddler, or at least not with me. I've gotten used to the chill of sleeping alone, even when there's someone else in the bed. So I was surprised when he pulled me into the crook of his arm, and amazed by how good it felt to be held.

"It's one of her student breakfasts," I mumbled into his chest.

"I'm sorry if I was too rough last night." He stroked my shoulder and whispered into my hair. "It's this damned new organic certification law."

"What's the problem?" My voice was muffled by the fabric of his pajama top.

"Last session we passed a law making it harder for farms to get certified organic. A measure to repeal it is coming up in the next regular session." He sighed and ran his hand through my hair. "Richardson wants a guarantee I'll vote to keep the law, and he's got all the big ag-money guys behind him. And the activist groups pushing for the repeal are a hodgepodge of hippies and eco-freaks who don't have a dime between them, which wouldn't be good for my reelection coffers. But I keep getting the troubling suspicion that they might be right. It's driving me crazy."

"If you agree with them, why not vote for the repeal?" I closed my eyes. Maybe we could fall asleep like this.

I could feel Jack shaking his head. "It might have been that simple back in your Ben Franklin's day, but I've got a campaign office to staff, and in another year I'll be running again. I can't afford to piss off the deep pockets."

I shifted and looked up at him. "What's the use of running for office if you don't get to vote your conscience? Although I'll grant you that even way back when, voting one's conscience wasn't always the best strategy for reelection. I was reading about Senator Humphrey Marshall the other day, and it didn't work so well for him. In 1795, a stone-throwing mob showed up outside his house when they didn't like his vote. But those were angry voters, not donors."

Jack chuckled. "I depend on you to give me historical perspective." He nudged my head down his chest. "How about a nightcap, Avi? Something to put me to sleep."

Right. So much for unsolicited cuddling. I wondered if Pete liked to snuggle.

Later, the taste of Jack on my tongue, I drifted off thinking about poor Senator Marshall and wondering what it would take to get angry mobs in the streets today.

Chapter Four

Sunlight streamed through the second-story windows and onto gleaming wooden tables. The air smelled of coffee, cheese, and toast. I limped into the restaurant on my crutches, fielded the predictable questions about my injury and settled into a chair by the window, figuring I'd let the others jockey for a seat next to Herself, the woman who presided over the head of the table like a silver-haired Nigerian queen.

Every few months, Professor Joan White buys breakfast for her covey of doctoral students. Prof Joan is one of the foremost authorities on Thomas Jefferson's descendants, both the legitimate white branch and the only recently acknowledged children he had with his wife's half sister, the slave Sally Hemings. I love Prof Joan. She's brilliant and tough, and of course it's an honor to work with her, but 6:00 a.m.?

The June breakfast, like the rest of the summer meetings, was small. Two of her students had defended the month before, one was on her way to a postdoctoral fellowship in Florida, and another would be slipping straight into a faculty job at some small college on the West Coast. Academic jobs were precious and rare, so we all expected to scatter across the country after graduation. There were six of us left, a diverse group of men and women from various ethnic backgrounds, all interested in some aspect of early American history.

The newest member of our group sat beside me. I tried to remember his name. Jose something? He looked at me. "You're Avi, right? Someone said you've been here the longest."

I tried not to wince. "Yeah, seven years."

His eyes widened. "Whoa, I was hoping to get out of here in three."

Across the table, Kristy McGuire—a petite blonde whose proposal to study the early life of Susan B. Anthony had recently been approved and who had been lobbying Prof Joan for my teaching assistantship almost from the day she arrived—smirked at Jose from across the table. "It all depends on how long you take to write your dissertation. Avi got through his qualifying exams before most of us entered college." She focused her catty little gaze on me. "That must be quite the tome you're writing."

Bitch. Damn, the whole academic competition thing was exhausting.

I shrugged. "I'm still researching. We all have our own process, Kristy." I ignored her sneer and turned to Jose. "What's your area of interest?"

He shrugged. "I'm not sure yet. I have plenty of class work ahead of me. But maybe something about the Mexican-American War. What's your dissertation about?"

I took a sip of coffee, glanced down the table, and noticed that Prof Joan was listening. "I'm interested in the debates, and the behind the scenes manipulation, among delegates of the Constitutional Congress."

From down the table, she boomed, "Our Avi is a classic historian who eschews identity politics. Never mind that as a gay Jew they wouldn't have let him in the door."

I inclined my head toward her. It was an argument we'd been having for years. "Perhaps. On the other hand, the issues they were debating—proportional representation, division of powers, the slave trade—laid the foundation for our freedoms. Or in the case of the decision to table abolition, continued oppression. Representative government is still our only hope for permanent change."

She lifted her eyebrows. "That's assuming the government isn't corrupt."

"Corruption is certainly part of the story." I shrugged. "Human beings are flawed, including politicians. That's why the system is important."

She nodded. "I look forward to reading your justification."

The conversation moved on. I concentrated on my cheese omelet. Corrupt politicians were my specialty. After all, not only did my studies include their influence on historical events, I'd been sleeping with one for the past couple of years.

As the gathering broke up, Prof Joan signaled for me to stay behind. When everyone was gone, she scooted into the seat next to mine.

I accepted a coffee refill from the waitress and turned to my adviser. "What's up?"

She folded her hands and rested her bangled wrists on the table. "I was putting together the teaching assistantship roster for next semester."

Breakfast churned nastily in my stomach. There are never enough teaching assistantships in the history department to keep all the graduate students fed and sheltered. I'd been lucky enough to get one almost every fall for the past seven years. The first five of those, I'd had to find part-time work in the spring to keep a roof over my head. Since I moved into Jack's apartment, I'd been able to make one semester's worth of stipend last through the year. I waited, hoping my foreboding was misguided.

"It's time you finished, Avi. Don't you agree?" In contrast to the rich brown of her skin, Prof Joan's pale green eyes could be unnerving, especially when she was about to tell me something unpleasant.

I nodded. "I'm hoping to defend in the spring."

She shook her head. "You said that last year and, I believe, the year before."

I started to speak, but she held up her hand. "I understand that you want it to be perfect, and I commend your carefulness, but eventually you have to put yourself out there."

I focused on a gouge mark in the table, praying this conversation would end soon. "I understand."

I could hear her nails tapping against her coffee cup. "It's my job to push you. I haven't been doing that very well." She waited until I looked up to continue. Her face had a firm but kind expression that made my gut clench. "There's no reason you can't defend in the fall, which means I will need to see a draft of your dissertation soon. I'm giving you until August fifteenth. If it's not on my desk by then, I'll withdraw your name from the teaching roster and give the job to Kristy."

I stared at her, wide-eyed. "You want me to write my dissertation this summer? I'm still gathering material."

She blew air out in an exasperated sound. "Avi, it's been years. If you can't write this up in a timely manner, you don't belong in academia."

I bit my lip, determined not to show any emotion.

She reached over and patted my arm. "You've done enough research. It's time to start writing. I'm confident you'll be able to get a draft done. You have almost three months." With that, she grabbed the check and stood. I watched her walk away. I wasn't going to panic. I laid my head down on the table and tried to keep myself from hyperventilating.

Holy shit, shit, shit.

* * * *

The next morning, I woke to an empty bed. I heard the rustle of papers from the kitchen. The other pillow still held the impression of Jack's head, and I could smell fresh-brewed coffee. I wondered how long he'd stay this time.

It's a sexist truth that there isn't a name for what I am to Jack. I can't be a mistress, so am I a mister? My official position is caretaker. In exchange for forwarding the mail, answering the phone, and generally taking care of the place while he's gone, Jack's campaign manager lets me camp out in the empty apartment. There's a second bedroom set up with twin beds for the boys, and, in theory, I sleep there or vacate the place whenever Jack's in town. Needless to say, I haven't spent a night in there, although I do move to Isaac's couch if Jack brings his wife, Peggy. Which doesn't happen very often since she likes to stay home with their kids.

When Jack and I were first together, I hated to see him go. Lately it's been much easier.

I rolled myself up and swung my legs off the bed. My ankle felt a little less stiff. I grabbed the crutches and hobbled toward the bathroom to shower, wondering vaguely what Pete would think of my situation. I shook my head and stepped into the shower. In my position, self-reflection wasn't always wise. I avoided it whenever possible.

By the time I got myself into the kitchen, Jack had finished breakfast and was stuffing papers into his briefcase. He looked up. "Morning, sleepyhead."

I imagined him using those exact words with his sons and shivered. There was a ten-year age difference between his eldest and me, and the same between Jack and my father. Not a pattern I liked to think about. Similarities between my rejecting father and my adulterous lover weren't associations I wanted to make.

I glanced at the wall clock—not yet seven. "Early meeting?"

"Richardson wants to get together before the committee meets. Get all our ducks in a row. How's The Project going?"

He pronounced it with an emphasis he must have picked up from me.

I found a cup and poured myself coffee. "Frustrating. And my adviser gave me an ultimatum yesterday. If I don't get a draft done by August, she won't renew my teaching assistantship, which means I might be out of a job."

"Fuck her." Jack reached into his pocket and brought out his cell phone. "I'll get my office to hire you. That way you can take all the time you need."

Sometimes he was a great guy. On the other hand, nothing was free, and I wasn't sure I wanted to sign on for a longer tour of duty. None of my self-justification made sense if I wasn't on my way to a real job somewhere else. "Thanks. I might take you up on that. In the meantime, maybe a deadline will help me finally finish the damned thing."

"You sure?" At my nod, he slid his phone back in place. "Say the word."

I sipped my coffee and watched him assemble himself to leave. "When will you be home? Should I get us some dinner?"

He shook his head. "It'll be late before I get back." He ran his hand down my spine and patted my ass. "Keep the bed warm for me."

I watched him walk out of the apartment, fixed my oatmeal and opened my laptop to read the *New York Times*.

Eventually I forced myself to close the paper and open The Project. I reread my last few paragraphs. Poppycock and balderdash. Academic bullshit when all I really wanted to write was that Ben Franklin had warned about money in politics way back in the first Constitutional Congress. It was indeed a dirty business. There'd been corruption, lies and blackmail from the beginning. Things hadn't changed much since then. But that would make for a very short dissertation and wouldn't earn me that gold star of a PhD. I made another pot of coffee and resolved to keep slogging away.

Around noon, my cell phone chittered with a text from Isaac. I hit *Save* on the laptop to preserve my pathetic morning ramblings and picked up the phone to call him. Maybe I could talk him into bringing over some beer, and we could piss away the afternoon.

* * * *

Jack would have killed me if he knew I invited anyone to the apartment. But since we didn't have real neighbors, how could he find out? It seemed like the nearby apartments passed from one philandering politician to another. And the elected representatives went out of their way to avoid the hallway and elevator if anyone else was there. At one point, there was a woman living down the hall whose place was frequented by a Republican from Racine. I hadn't seen her since a few months after I moved in, although I still glimpsed him around every now and then. As far as I could tell, I was the only full-time resident on my floor.

So I didn't worry about Jack's disapproval when, an hour later, the door buzzed and there stood Isaac, six-pack in hand.

"You're a saint." I opened the door wide for him.

"Heart of gold, that's me." He stared at my crutches. "What happened to you?"

I mumbled something about a tree and closed the door behind him. I wanted to wait until we were settled with beers before I brought up Pete, wanted to keep him a secret for a few moments longer. And at the same time, I really wanted to talk.

He glanced around the apartment. "The assemblyman's in town? I take it you're not expecting him home anytime soon."

I nodded and hobbled toward the couch. Secrets. When did I get so comfortable with them? Jack and me—there was a big one. How my thoughts kept circling around Pete was another. And Jack would be appalled if he found out that Isaac had been to the apartment and knew about him. But then Isaac had his own set of secrets.

"He's in meetings through dinner."

Isaac strolled to the refrigerator and peered in. "And what did he expect you to eat? There's nothing in here but condiments and milk." He pulled out two beer bottles and shoved the rest of the pack into the fridge.

He brought me a beer. I took it with a nod of thanks. "I went to the store day before yesterday, but with my foot I couldn't carry much back. There's some frozen crap. I'll be okay."

He shook his head, folding himself into a chair across from me. "Make me a list, and I'll pick up whatever you need. Nate's gonna be down at the lake lab all afternoon so I don't have anything else to do."

As always, Isaac's face glowed as he mentioned Nathan—once his teacher and now his lover—the man who loved him in spite of his past. Some nights, when I woke up in a sweat thinking about my own moral choices, the story of Isaac and Nathan gave me hope.

I threw Isaac a coaster. The last thing I wanted was to have to explain water rings on the furniture. "Actually, I was thinking I'd stop by the farmers' market tomorrow, buy some healthy food."

Isaac gestured toward my foot. "You're kidding, right?"

I shrugged. "I sort of met someone."

He stared at me.

I propped my foot on the couch, suddenly self-conscious, and changed the subject. "Didn't you just get back from visiting Nathan's mom in Chicago?"

He nodded. "Nate's mom is great. I swear, we should all have a mother like that."

I took a pull of beer, relishing the crisp taste of dry lager. "Yeah, mine tries hard, but I can't imagine her inviting my lover to her birthday party." I pictured Pete at my mom's kitchen table and wondered if his smile would win her over eventually. But that was crazy thinking. I focused again on what Isaac was saying.

"Now imagine that the boyfriend she's inviting home used to make his living on his back and is seventeen years younger than your son." Isaac propped his feet on the coffee table. I gestured for him to put them down. I didn't feel like cleaning before Jack got home.

He shook his head and put his feet back on the floor.

I saluted him with my beer. "You're selling yourself short. You're a great guy, and Nathan's lucky to have you. So what if you paid for your undergraduate education in an unorthodox way? We all do what we have to, to get by."

He took a long swig of beer. "Thanks. I feel the same way about you."

I frowned. Much as I prided myself on feeling nonjudgmental toward Isaac, I didn't like it when he acted like we were brothers under the skin. After all, it wasn't like I had sex with strangers. I cleared my throat. "I do care about him, you know."

Isaac nodded. "And as I've told you before, it would be easier if you didn't."

We drank in silence for a few minutes. Eventually Isaac said, "Let's back up. You met someone at the farmers' market?"

I glanced toward the crutches, feeling bashful. "His name's Pete. He has a booth."

"And?"

I adjusted my foot, trying to get comfortable. I paused, savoring the image of Pete, his smile, those sexy hands as he passed me his card. "And he gave me his number."

Isaac's eyebrows rose. "Are you going to call? What about Assemblyman Foots-the-Bill?"

I shrugged. "It's not like we pledged monogamy. I mean, the man has a wife."

He cocked his head and considered me. "That doesn't necessarily mean he'd be fine with you getting fucked by someone else."

I looked away, feeling uneasy under Isaac's gaze. "Maybe. I wouldn't need to tell him."

Isaac gave me a look.

I played with my beer bottle. "Yeah, well, I probably won't call Pete anyway."

"Right. Why call when you can stop by his booth?" Isaac sighed. "Your business, not mine. But be careful. My experience is that people are very particular about getting what they're paying for, and I'm betting your assemblyman thinks he's buying exclusive rights."

"It's not like that." I tried not to sound exasperated. We'd had this argument too many times before. "Jack and I are in a relationship. Participating in an extramarital affair doesn't make me a prostitute."

"Honey, you keep telling yourself that if it makes you feel better." Isaac strolled toward the kitchen. He came back waving the bottle of single malt scotch the governor gave Jack for Christmas. "When do we get to taste this?"

I shook my head. "Never. Jack's wife wants him to save it for a special occasion."

Isaac set the bottle on the coffee table. He looked around the apartment. "I've heard of house-sitting gigs that were better than this."

I scowled.

He shrugged and took it back. He returned with two beers. "Let's change the subject. Tell me all about how your dissertation is going, and I'll whine about life as a teaching assistant."

I groaned. "Don't make me talk about The Project. Anything but that."

He handed me another beer. "Energy Systems Lab whining it is, then."

Chapter Five

The Wednesday market was smaller and closer to my apartment. Jack intended to stay in town for another day, which meant the last thing I should do was limp to the market to flirt with Pete. And yet, after Jack left the apartment, I did a few rounds of the alphabet with my toes, rewrapped my ankle, shrugged into the same backpack I'd taken to get groceries a few days before and started the three-block walk. Since I was already feeling guilty, I might as well go ahead and see Pete. And a little flirtation never hurt anyone, right?

Ten in the morning and already the air felt thick. The *click* and *clomp* of my crippled gait was smothered by the grind of a bus changing gears on the hill. Sweat dripped down my back as I climbed in the direction of the Capitol Square. It would be a good day to stay inside with the air conditioner blasting. And to write the fucking first chapter, unless I wanted to let the masculine form of mistress slide completely into kept man.

At the crest of the hill, I paused to adjust my shirt, which kept bunching around the crutch pads at my armpits. I ran my fingers through my hair, sure cowlicks were sprouting from humidity and sweat. It occurred to me that I might have exaggerated Pete's attractiveness, that my subconscious might have endowed him with more sex appeal in those furtive moments when I fingered his business card.

A few blocks ahead, a line of orange cones barred traffic from the side street. Near the barriers, an elderly black man played haunting blues on a tenor saxophone. I wondered if Jack, ensconced in the Capitol building, could hear the sax.

Pete's stall was near the middle of the blocked-off street. He seemed to be alone, and I wondered if Logan only helped on Saturdays. Despite the awning, sun streamed across one side of his table, and he'd piled his produce deeper on the shaded side, leaving flowers and a bin of potatoes in the sun. I stood for a few minutes watching as he laughed with one customer and bagged food for another. Too far away to hear the conversation, I noticed his smile, the easy confidence of his movements. He was even more attractive than I remembered.

The thought of his open proposition sent a surge of energy through me, dampened only by the way I could feel the Capitol looming behind me. It was like one of those mirror tricks: the mistress takes a mistress going on into infinity. Except *mistress* wasn't the right word. *Gigolo* didn't fit either. I was a man without a title, and I didn't want to think too hard about why I wanted Pete so much. Was it to prove Jack didn't own me? I hoped to hell it had more to do with Pete's smile than with Jack trying to control me, or Isaac calling me a whore.

Pete's dark blue tee, JAKOBSEN'S FARMS stenciled on the front, fit snugly around his upper arms and chest and bagged at the waist. He'd tied a rainbow-colored scarf at his neck. As I got closer, I noticed the matching band around his wrist. I was almost in front of the stand before he spotted me, his face breaking into a grin.

"Hi." The day seemed to brighten around him.

"Hey." I rested on my crutches, Pete's crutches. "How's it going?"

"Better now that you're here." Pete's gaze lingered on mine for a couple of breaths before he pulled a folding chair from the back of the stall and set it in the shade beside the table. "Have a seat. Did you walk?"

I nodded and gratefully slumped into the chair. "It's not far."

"Everywhere's a long way on crutches." Pete reached into a cooler at his feet and produced a red aluminum bottle that glistened with sweat. He unscrewed the top and handed it to me. Our fingers brushed in passing and I felt a zing of excitement.

I tipped it up and drank. The water was sweet and cold. "That's good."

He watched me, his eyes warm. "Well water from the farm."

A young woman sporting long braids and a baby in a papoose on her back interrupted us. "Do you have any basil?"

Pete pointed down the street. "Sorry, try the stall at the end. She usually has herbs." He turned back to me. "I'm in town and free this afternoon. You available?"

I glanced toward the Capitol. The portico shone in the sun. I seriously weighed inviting him back to the apartment. Who knew when Jack would be back? But that was the point. I couldn't be sure we wouldn't be caught, and I wasn't ready to test my theory of a non-monogamous relationship with Jack just yet. That was a gamble I was pretty sure I'd lose, and lose big. "Um, this isn't a good time."

Pete followed my gaze. "I see. Exactly how open is this relationship of yours?" I started to speak, but he waved me away. "Never mind. I don't think I want you to answer that."

He started bagging carrots for a customer without his usual smile.

"I'm sorry." I watched his strong, tan hands gently handling the food. I reached toward him but let my hand fall before it met his arm. "It's complicated."

He gave a short nod and counted out change for the middle-aged woman who was watching us like we were contestants on a reality show.

I stood, waited until she'd paid and gone before gesturing to my backpack. "I'd better get going, but I thought I'd pick up some produce. What do you recommend?"

He rested one hand on a hip and looked at me. "There's a lot of good stuff on offer here." He paused, letting that sink in before he continued, "But how about some peas and strawberries for starters."

He looked so gorgeous with his tee tight across his biceps and chest, his slim hips, his... I swallowed. "That all sounds good. I'll take the produce now, and maybe I can pick up the rest later."

He cocked his head, his gaze sliding down me in a way that made me shiver. "I wouldn't wait too long. It's always best when it's fresh."

* * * *

Jack opened the refrigerator, no doubt looking for a beer. He glanced at me. "There's real food in here. Turning over a new leaf?"

I kept my face blank. "Yeah, the surgeon general recommends fruits and veggies. I thought I'd give it a try and walked up to the farmers' market."

"Good for you." Jack surveyed the refrigerator. He pulled out a carton of strawberries and examined it. "Jakobsen's Farms. You meet the owner? He usually works the booth. A pain in the ass, but easy on the eyes."

My heart pounded. I stared into the distance for a moment, trying to look like I was struggling to remember. "Tall, blond, muscular type?"

Jack put the berries back in the refrigerator. "More like tenacious-terrier type. Once he gets his teeth in you, he never lets go. I get e-mails from him or one of his buddies almost every day. I swear, that man would do anything to get the new organic law revoked."

I shuffled through the stack of research articles I'd been organizing. "I still don't understand the issue. Why would organic farmers be against stricter rules?"

Jack pulled a beer from the refrigerator and sat in the chair across from me. "Because the new law makes it much more expensive to get certified, and most of these farms are struggling anyway. They argue that the federal rules are stringent enough."

"Are they?"

He took a long pull from his beer before answering. "Maybe. I told you, those hippies are probably right. That's part of why I find Jakobsen annoying."

I could feel him watching me thumb through my work. When he spoke again, his voice had dropped an octave. "Why don't you stop what you're doing, come over here, and suck me off?"

I looked up. He sat on the kitchen chair with his legs spread wide, one hand holding his beer bottle, the other nestled in the crook of his leg as if pointing toward his crotch. Was it my imagination, or was Jack getting more demanding every day? Dominance and submission wasn't where I would have taken our relationship, but I prided myself on my sexual flexibility. I'd never turned him down, wasn't sure what would happen if I did. Did that mean Isaac was right that the difference between us had to do with quantity, not quality? I didn't want to think about that any more than I wanted to test Jack's patience. I put down my papers and hobbled around the table to kneel between his legs. It was impossible to find a comfortable position for my ankle. I tried to ignore the persistent throb and ran my hands up his thighs.

He brushed a hand through my hair. "You're such a good boy." He grasped my hand and pressed it against his erection. "Aren't you?"

My eyelid twitched involuntarily. I focused on freeing Jack's impressive erection and tried to muster some enthusiasm for the task. Maybe if I gave him my best blowjob, I could ease off my ankle and get some more work done before bedtime.

* * * *

Jack left Friday morning, announcing he planned to drive straight home to Eagle River after work, but that he'd call when he knew his schedule for the next week. I stuffed the hundred dollars he left on the kitchen table into my wallet and tried not to feel like a whore. Outside, the rain poured, smearing across the window like tears.

I worked through the supporting material for Chapter Two until my eyes crossed. It was clear there were several holes in my argument, and I needed to get to the library to find evidence to patch them up. I glanced at the crutches leaning against the doorway and started cramming things into my backpack as if I were going on safari—laptop, notebooks, dry tennis shoes, a sweatshirt in case I stayed late on campus. On my bike, the trip down State Street took ten minutes tops, and that's if I hit every red light. But like Pete said, everywhere was a long way on crutches.

I shouldered my pack, pulled on rain boots, and draped myself in the long rain poncho my mother had insisted on sending with me freshman year, and which I'd worn exactly three times since, preferring my overpriced European black trench coat and giant umbrella to walking around in a big yellow circus tent. On the other hand, I didn't relish showing up at the library looking like a flood victim. I made sure the poncho covered my pack and left the apartment, feeling like one of those intrepid British naturalists who littered historical accounts of life in the eighteenth century. But of course, I was being more ridiculous than brave, girding myself to greet twenty-first-century Madison on crutches in the rain.

I waited in the apartment building lobby until the worst of the downpour abated. In Madison, rain tended to sweep through like a curtain, and it was sometimes possible to wait it out. As I stepped out of the door, I was struck by how clean my street smelled. Rather than hot pavement and bus fumes, I inhaled the fresh scent of rain-wet dirt. I trudged the extra block to a sheltered bus stop. Who knew when the torrent would wash through again?

It's awkward to hobble up bus steps and fumble for fare without dropping a crutch. I managed it and flopped onto one of the front seats reserved for handicapped riders. The hydraulic doors shut with a *hiss*, and the bus started chugging up the hill. The inside of the bus had that cozy rainy-day feel, the air redolent with diesel fumes and wet clothes. The bus bounced around the Capitol and down State Street, easing to the curb to allow on wet students, burned-out hippies, and the homeless.

I got off across from the quad and limped my way into the Historical Society, past the exhibit of weird things John Muir invented when he was here, like a rotating desk set to start at sunrise when sunlight passed through a lens and burned a thread, starting an improbable cascade of events that ended by presenting books and turning pages in a precisely timed order so he could finish his studies before breakfast. I'd seen him described as real-life steampunk. I hobbled up the stairs and into the library proper, hoping somewhere in the archives of important papers and historical treatises I'd find the solution to all my intellectual problems.

I loved libraries, especially those that housed old books. They were quiet, dusty smelling and safe. The archive research room, with its dark paneling, wooden tables and bright fluorescent lights, felt like centuries colliding, and it gave me peace to inhale that distinctive old-book scent, which I was told comes from deteriorating paper, silverfish feces and dust.

My first love was Abraham Lincoln. My peculiar upbringing meant that the first time I read anything substantive about the sixteenth president I was thirteen, the odd boy in a new school. Abe was a gawky-looking hero with sad eyes and dark hair who had my name—Avi is short for Avraham— and I was dying to make the leap from Hebrew to English. Entranced by a past different from the one I'd been living in, I threw myself into my eighth-grade American history class. From Lincoln, I moved backward to the Founding Fathers, a phrase that captured me, perhaps because it sounded like Our Forefathers, about whom I'd studied in yeshiva, which made it seem comforting and heretical at the same time. Or maybe it was simply that I was drawn to any father other than my own.

I glanced at the clock and texted Isaac to see if he wanted to meet me in a few hours for a beer after he finished teaching. He was a reference center of a different sort. As always, the ancient government documents calmed me. There was something soothing about the feel of old paper and the rhythm of formal language. I lost myself in the texts. By the time Isaac's class ended and he texted me back, I felt like everything might be okay.

He said he'd meet me at the union. I shut down my laptop, gathered my photocopies, returned the originals to a reference librarian and hobbled downstairs. Water dripped from gutters, and cars splashed through puddles, but the drenching rain had passed, replaced by a fine mist. I crossed the street to the student union, which was crowded and noisy compared to the quiet of the library. An old building, the hallways smelled of stale fried food and furniture polish.

I made my way down to the Rathskeller, where the temperature rose as bodies teemed toward the bar. The place always struck me as a little creepy, with rough wooden arches and old-fashioned murals, complete with slogans in German, covering the walls. Isaac waved to me from one end of a long wooden table and gestured toward the pitcher of amber beer and two full glasses before him. I maneuvered to him, glad not to have to fling myself into the press of undergraduates at the bar.

He pushed a beer toward me as I slid onto the bench across from him, tucking my crutches beside me like a friend. "Hey, how's the eighteenth century?"

"Simpler, I think." I took a grateful swallow of the bitter brew.

"Probably not for the likes of us." Isaac watched me over the rim of his glass. "Although you seem to like things complicated these days."

I laughed. "That's the excuse I keep giving Pete. "'It's complicated.'"

"It isn't really." Isaac leaned back, sipping his beer. "For a while now, you've been getting more and more disillusioned with Jack. Otherwise you wouldn't be tempted to take up with Pete."

I frowned at him, feeling pushed. I sure as hell wasn't ready to move on from Jack, not with my skinny bank account. "Thank you, Mr. Convert to Monogamy. The one doesn't necessarily follow the other. An affair can just mean you're horny."

He nodded. "Sure it can. And I didn't say everyone who fucks someone outside their primary relationship is expressing dissatisfaction. But you are. Pete can't be the first offer you've had in two years."

"Of course not." I crossed my arms over my chest and surveyed the room. Late afternoon brought people to the bar in groups. "Do you know what the story is behind all the murals?"

He glanced at the wall beside us. "No. But I'm willing to change the subject if you want. How's The Project coming?"

I shrugged. We sat silently. I spun my beer glass around on the table, letting it slide through its wet spot. "When you were working, did you ever get into any bondage stuff?"

He knit his eyebrows together. "The assemblyman likes to play?"

I nodded.

Isaac took a long breath. "How about you?"

I bit my lip. "I mean, I'm not against it or anything, for anyone else anyway. But it doesn't do it for me. Really doesn't do it, if you know what I mean."

Isaac refilled our glasses. "In answer to your question, I wasn't that guy. Like any other field, everyone has their areas of expertise. That wasn't mine." I gave him an inquisitive look. He shook his head. "And that's all I'm going to say about that. But my impression is that you need to be careful. Especially if you're a top."

I took a long gulp of beer and refilled it again. I held up my glass. "Here's to expertise. Let's hope Jack has it." I drained it.

Isaac rested a hand on my forearm. A couple of frat boys looked at us, and he pulled back. I wanted to whine at them that we were just friends, like that would keep us from getting our faces smashed.

Our pitcher was almost gone, and I split the rest between our glasses. I chugged my beer and whispered, "Let's leave."

Eyeing the frat boys, Isaac frowned. "I'm meeting Nathan here in a few minutes. The people he works with at the lake lab like to get together for a beer after work on Friday afternoons."

I blinked at him, realizing it had been a long time since I mixed work and pleasure. "Have you met them? I mean, do they know you're together?"

"Of course I've met them. And why wouldn't they know we were together?" He frowned. "You think they're going to shun him for being gay? They're serious scientists. They don't care who he's fucking. The only thing that matters for them is whether he's easy to work with and if he's good in boats. And maybe his publication record."

Why was I surprised? Except for the boats, that's how it was in the history department too. "It's only that men his age…" I stopped at the look on Isaac's face. "Sorry, I mean—"

He waved his hand like he was brushing away cobwebs. "Not everyone in their forties is a politician. You want to hang out with us? Usually the group eventually goes out for Thai food. If you're broke, I can spot you some cash."

I thought of the hundred in my wallet. Maybe a night out was exactly what I needed.

The decibel level in the room rose, and Nathan—a handsome, middle-aged man in worn jeans and a T-shirt—was swept to the table in the middle of a pack of laughing bronzed giants, or so it seemed until I looked closer and realized that with their tans and air of outdoorsy vigor, Nathan's giants were much like any other group of twentysomethings. A thin redhead with wire-rimmed glasses collected five-dollar bills as the group wrangled over beer choices. Nathan's hand rested on Isaac's shoulder in greeting, while the stream of cheerful, healthy people settled in a thick barrier between us and the frat boys. I liked Nathan's friends immediately and dug out a five for the pot.

Nathan extended his hand across the table to shake mine before he slid onto the bench, next to Isaac. "Avi, how nice to see you. How's your ankle?"

I gestured toward the crutches. "I'm almost mobile."

A broad-shouldered, brunette woman settled beside me. "I'm Callie. Are you a friend of Nathan and Isaac?" She sounded British.

I shook the hand she offered.

Nathan looked at her warmly. "Callie's an organizing fool. If you're not careful, you'll find yourself on a committee to overthrow the university."

She chortled. "Hardly. But are you in the teaching assistants' union?"

Isaac wiggled his eyebrows at me. "Avi tries to stay away from modern-day politics. He finds it punishing."

I gave him a look and turned to Callie. "I don't even know if I'll be teaching in the fall."

"Are you in engineering with Isaac?" She poured a glass of stout from one of the pitchers that were being passed from hand to hand and gestured toward my empty glass.

I slid my glass toward Nathan, who was pouring something paler. "History. Early American."

"To the early Americans." Callie clinked glasses with me and took a long sip. "God, that tastes good. I've been crunching numbers all day, and I'm dead ready to relax and think about something else."

"Here's to escaping the crap." Isaac held my gaze as he lifted his glass. "And doing whatever it takes."

I raised my glass, wondering which he was suggesting, escaping or doing whatever it took? And which did I want? Yet another question I didn't want to answer. The table was dotted with pitchers of beer, each a slightly different hue. I gulped half my glass and considered which I'd try next. A man could easily get drunk on five-dollar pitchers shared with friends.

Chapter Six

Miraculously I woke without a hangover the next morning. Saturday. I told myself that it would be good exercise to walk to the market, that I shouldn't stay cooped up. I tried not to notice how carefully I was dressing for a casual stroll through the Saturday market.

The air felt cool and pleasant, but I could tell that soon enough the thick, humid June heat would make me glad to escape into an air-conditioned apartment. I lurched the blocks to the market, that fresh-as-a-daisy, post shower feeling disintegrating along the way.

The early-morning crowd was relatively easy to navigate through. People congregated around the coffee cart. Smells assailed me as I made my way through the first couple of blocks of stalls—the heavy floral tones of cut flowers, yeasty bread and cinnamon from a bakery stall, the distinctive fragrance of tomato plants.

I turned the corner, my heart rate increasing as I neared Pete's stall. I stopped to watch him weighing beans for an elderly couple. With his hair a curly blond halo and his skin a radiant golden brown, Pete looked like the sun itself. The old man he was serving pushed a three-wheeled walker, which was doubling as a grocery cart. Pete leaned over the table to deposit the plastic bag of beans in the walker's pouch. He moved with gentleness, a big man being careful around infirmity. All the while he talked and smiled. I could hear a reflection of his kindness in the old woman's laugh and felt my own armor cracking, like an easing of tight muscles around my chest.

Logan saw me first. He nudged Pete and pointed. Pete turned, our eyes met, and I started my awkward swing toward him.

"Hey." I stopped a few feet from the booth.

He gestured toward my foot. "How's the ankle?"

I shrugged and lifted the crutches. "Better. I'm afraid I may need to keep these a while longer. I can't get very far without them yet."

He shook his head. "No problem. They were collecting dust in the barn anyway."

Our eyes locked. I could feel my chest warming, loosening. Not to mention the heat that look was producing in other parts of my body. I leaned toward him, like a plant toward the sun. It felt inevitable.

I cleared my throat. "Do you want to get dinner or something sometime?"

His smile widened. "I'm free tonight. I know a great Italian place on the East Side. I could meet you there about seven."

I gestured toward my swollen ankle. "You'd better pick me up. My only transport is a broken bike."

He nodded and held my gaze until a young couple with a stroller elbowed their way past me and started asking about the peas.

I turned and started back the way I came, smiling like a jack-o'-lantern and wondering what the hell I was doing.

* * * *

I opened the passenger door as soon as the old truck pulled to the curb, handed the crutches to Pete, and swung up onto the passenger seat.

Pete's eyes sparkled. "You look great."

I considered him. "You do too." And he did, scrubbed clean, in khaki chinos and a white button-down that set off his tan, his blond curls wild around his face, more like California than Wisconsin. He shifted into gear, and I found myself riveted by the size and strength of his hand on the shift.

You'd think I never got laid. I forced myself to watch the neighborhood passing by. "So, how'd it go today? You sell everything?"

Pete laughed. "Almost. It was a good day. This hot guy stopped by and asked me out."

"Yeah? Good thing I got there first."

He snorted. "Right."

The restaurant was in an undistinguished storefront in the middle of a strip mall, with a nail parlor on one side and office space on the other. The inside was dimly lit, the air heavy with mouthwatering aromas. A teenage hostess in too much makeup led us to a corner table set with a red-checkered tablecloth, white carnations and a flickering candle in a red glass orb.

I looked around, taking in the ancient travel posters decorating the walls. "This place is like something out of a movie."

Pete nodded. "I know. Isn't it wild? And the food's good too."

I watched him perusing the menu, his square jaw even more handsome in candlelight. The whole scene was patently, cheesily romantic, a first date straight out of 1950, except of course for the lack of gender diversity at the table.

Romantic. I guess I could do that.

"If a trio comes over to serenade us, I'm out of here." I opened my menu. "How's the Alfredo?"

"Wonderfully artery clogging. No serenading, noted. You want wine?"

I glanced at him over my menu. "The house red has to be Chianti in a place like this. How could we drink anything else?"

In the end, we ordered too much food and a carafe of fruity red wine.

First dates—a weird phenomenon where both people spent the night trying to be charming and wondering how it would end. In this case, I was pretty sure I knew the answer to that. Pete didn't seem the shrinking violet type. And yet nervousness hummed between us, as palpable as the sexual tension that was making my face flush and my cock stir.

It had been a long time since I'd really wanted anyone. Pete's hands flew while he told a funny anecdote about a dog getting loose in the market. Barely following the thread of the story, I watched the muscles rippling along his biceps and his lips forming the words and pictured what those arms and that mouth might be doing in a few hours. I laughed at the punch line, feeling stupid with desire.

The food came. Pete asked me about teaching. I lost myself in the conversation for a few minutes. Then he leaned forward, and I wondered if he was also caught by the pulse between us. After that, all I wanted was for dinner to end so we could get on with the main course.

"Can I interest you gentlemen in dessert?" The waiter gathered our plates and silver.

Pete raised his eyebrows and looked at me.

My mouth went dry.

His eyes never left mine. "I think we'll get that ourselves."

The waiter shuffled off, looking uncomfortable. He brought back the bill. I reached for it, but Pete got there first, and I felt guilty at my relief. I probably should have insisted. After all, I asked him out. But my wallet was pretty damned thin.

Pete smiled at me as he slid money into the fake leather sleeve. "I picked the restaurant." He let his gaze drift down to my mouth. "Besides, I'm feeling lucky."

By the time I climbed into his truck, my sex drive was at full throttle.

Pete turned to me, resting his hand on my thigh. "I live a twenty-minute drive away in a small farmhouse with my sister and her son. Can we go to your place?"

I hesitated. Jack wouldn't like it. Whatever he might feel about my having sex with another man—and I didn't want to think about that—I was very certain he'd think taking him home would be too dangerous. And Jack might be right. It hadn't taken Isaac more than five minutes to figure it all out. But Isaac saw the world through jaded glasses.

Pete slid his hand higher on my thigh, and I nodded. "My place is fine."

He gave me that toothy smile, like a fucking toothpaste commercial. He moved his hand from my thigh, and I almost groaned in disappointment.

Pete shifted into first gear and started toward my apartment. "I take it that means you don't live with this guy you're having an open relationship with."

I shifted in my seat, cradling the crutches between my legs. "I don't really want to talk about him, if that's all right with you."

Pete shrugged. "Works for me. I've never been into threesomes."

We were nearing the apartment building. I gestured toward the driveway. "We have a spot in back. You can park there."

He turned the wheel. "Right. I won't ask about the 'we.'"

"I'm a caretaker. The owner's not in town right now." I directed him into the spot. As I led Pete in through the back door, I couldn't help feeling ridiculous, swinging from crutches as he walked behind. Under normal circumstances, I'd have been conscious of how my ass moved. It would have been part of the seduction to let him see the ripple of muscles as I walked. Harder to do suspended between poles.

I gestured toward the security cameras circling the lobby. Pete nodded, and we waited for the elevator, both of us facing the paneled door. Pete brushed his knuckles along my arm, sending bolts of sensation spiraling up my arm and down my spine to my stiffening cock. The door opened on an empty elevator.

I stepped in and pushed the button. Pete followed, glancing around. "This place has great security."

"Yeah, even in the hallways."

"Good to know." He leaned against the back wall of the elevator, watching the door. "Safety is important."

The elevator door opened, and I led Pete down the hall to Jack's apartment, wondering if that was true.

Pete stood close behind me as I fitted the key in the lock. His breath felt warm against my neck. He smelled of diesel and shampoo. Even though we didn't touch, I felt him like a pulse on my back. It took forever for me to unlock the apartment. The door swung open, and he followed me in, kicking it closed behind him.

And we were alone, no cameras or waiters to keep us from touching. We stood staring at each other for a heartbeat. He stepped forward, his arms encircling my waist. I wrapped my arms around his neck, and the crutches fell to the floor with a clatter. I had to tilt my head to kiss him. He opened to my tongue, his mouth a hot cavern I wanted to explore.

Pete tasted of tomato and wine. It had been a long time since I kissed anyone. Jack didn't kiss, and I'd gotten used to sex without the slow roll of lips and teeth and tongues. I couldn't get over how good Pete tasted, how sexy it was to twine my tongue around his.

He moved his hands down my back, and I pressed myself into him, groaning as he kneaded the flesh of my ass. My cock throbbed, and I felt him hard against me. I started pulling at his shirt, wanting more than anything to feel his skin next to mine.

He broke the kiss and slid his lips along my jawline. "We should get you off your ankle." His breath tickled against my neck.

"Bedroom." I gestured with my head, and Pete pressed a kiss into my neck that almost melted my knees. "Now."

He shifted sideways and looped his arm under my shoulder. "Lean on me, Gimpy. I'll get you to bed."

I laughed and limped with him toward the bedroom. "I'm sure this is sexy."

"You have no idea." He ran his free hand down my chest and belly to caress the cock straining to be free of my pants. "Of course, it's been a long time."

"Ah, a man who's lowered his standards. Must be my lucky day."

"Hardly." He helped me onto the bed. We pulled our shirts off, and I found myself facing his bare torso. A trail of sandy blond hair led down from his belly button to his belt. I stared for a moment at the bulge below and reached to trace the outline of him pressing through his pants. Pete groaned, and I dived forward, tasting the salty sweetness of his skin while I stroked his shaft through the cloth with one hand and worked his belt with the other. Little moans escaped from him as he rested his hands on my shoulders and rocked against me.

I pulled back to see him as I peeled down his pants. His cock thrust out at me, cut with an appealing upward curve. A drop glistened on the slit. I looked up at Pete, who was standing very still, watching me, his lower lip caught in his teeth. I held his gaze and flicked my tongue over the tip. He gasped, and his mouth fell open. He tasted like salted cream. I wrapped my hand around him. His skin was smooth and hot. I took him in, the head of his cock firm and round in my mouth. I closed my eyes and gave myself over to the feel of his dick in my hand and mouth. His sweat smelled musky and yet fresh, like newly mowed hay.

"Wait." Pete stopped me. "I want to feel you too."

I blinked up at him, so used to being the one to service that it took a moment before I understood. Meanwhile, he kicked out of his pants and shoes and pushed me back on the bed. The sheets smelled like Jack. I pressed my eyes closed, willing away a flicker of guilt. When I opened them, I saw Pete bending over me, unsnapping my jeans. Propping myself on my elbows, I watched while he stripped off the rest of my clothing, grateful for the care he took with my injured ankle. Jack was home with Peggy. It was my turn to feel good. I scooted back on the bed, and Pete slid up my body, his skin delicious against mine.

He kissed me, his tongue claiming mine, his kiss banishing Jack and demanding all my attention. He curled his hand around my cock and felt incredibly good. I reached between us and found him, hot, hard and wet from my mouth. He pressed his thigh between my legs, the pressure against my balls an exquisite agony, and stroked me in a ragged, infuriating, exhilarating rhythm that had me gasping into his mouth. He brushed his fingers across my nipple and I shivered. He flicked it harder, and I arched into him. It felt like he was everywhere, and I was falling into his mouth, his hands, his cock, his skin, his sweat, his heat, his breath, his moan in my mouth, the thrusts he slid along my palm, his hot seed spilling onto my belly, me following fast as the waves rolled through and I crashed against him while he held me tight, his heart and cock pulsing with mine.

We lay together, our breaths coming in gulps, our hearts gradually slowing.

Eventually Pete propped himself on an elbow and looked down at me. "And that's with you injured. God help me when your ankle heals." He must have seen hesitation in my eyes, because he added, "Or maybe you were thinking this is a onetime thing."

I shook my head and looked up into those dark blue eyes. "It's not that. But I never know when I'm going to be, well, free."

He rolled off me and sat. "Right. The guy, the one who's not in bed with us. Sorry, I'd completely forgotten about him."

So had I. Resting my hand on his hip, I realized how much I wanted Pete there. Jack or no Jack.

Pete ran a hand through his hair, and his blond curls sprang out at wild angles. "I really don't know the etiquette here, but I suppose that's my cue to leave."

The apartment seemed to swell with more than the average loneliness of a Saturday night. I grabbed his hand. "Don't go, Pete. Please, stay."

He stared down at me, and I lost myself in his eyes again. A smile flickered at the edge of his lips. He ran a finger along my collarbone and tapped my sternum. "You're dangerous."

I sat up to take his face in my hands and kiss him slowly, a languid promise that tasted of our mouths together.

When it broke, he whispered into my mouth, "Ask me again."

I pushed him onto his back, my body following his down like a magnet, and caressed the hard line of his jaw. He looked into my eyes, his expression soft but a little wary. I whispered, "Can you stay the night?"

His gaze grazed across my face like he was memorizing my features. When our lips touched, I sank into their softness. He opened to me, and I slid my tongue in, rolling against his in a slow, sexy dance.

I broke and looked down at him. He smiled, making little circles on my back with his hand.

I touched the hard line across his bicep where pale skin turned dark. "Farmer's tan."

He glanced down, his laugh a little self-conscious. "Occupational hazard. Sorry, I know it's not very appealing, but there hasn't been anyone looking in a long time."

I fingered the ropes of muscle along his upper arm. I let my gaze travel down the length of his strong, lean body. "You're very appealing. Which makes me wonder why no one's been looking."

Pete shrugged. "Where would I meet someone? Buying chicken feed at the farmers' co-op? Or maybe the monthly Southeast Wisconsin Organic Agriculture meeting?"

"You meet thousands of people at the farmers' market."

He smiled. "True, but you'd be surprised how rarely gorgeous men fall at my feet there. Most people only stop by for the lettuce."

Absentmindedly I traced my initials in the soft blond hair of his chest. Glancing toward Jack's closet, I wiped my hand across his chest, erasing. "There are the bars."

He cocked an eyebrow. "Are you trying to get rid of me?"

I shook my head. "No. Just wondering why you're doing the lonely Norwegian bachelor farmer thing."

He laughed. "Danish, actually, on my dad's side. American mixed on my mom's. And the bar scene doesn't exactly fit with the farming lifestyle, you know. In bed by nine, up with the dawn."

I glanced at the clock. "It's past ten now."

"Doesn't matter. I paid Logan twenty bucks to do my morning chores tomorrow. Best investment I've made in a long time." He pulled me into another long, delicious kiss.

I felt his cock thickening against my hip. My own stirred, awakening like a sleepy serpent. With one hand, Pete held the back of my neck, while the other roamed down my spine. I straddled him, and our still-sticky cocks brushed, the touch an electric jolt that brought a groan from Pete. He slid his hands down my sides to cradle my hips, his thumbs caressing the creases of my thighs. Need flared, and I braced myself against the bed and thrust, angling my cock to lick against his and ignoring the twinges of pain in my ankle. His tongue pushed against mine, his mouth opening as I moved. His breath quickened. His thumbs were furrowing the creases in my thighs, brushing into my pubic hairs and gliding back out in rhythm with each long sweep I made of my cock against his. We were both rock hard. Sweat slicked the space between us. The air smelled of sex.

I winced as my foot caught on the sheets and pain shot up my leg.

Pete twisted beneath me, and I slid sideways onto the bed, my weight falling on my good leg, my hurt ankle hovering in the air before gently settling beside its mate.

"You okay?" He asked, rolling onto his side above me.

"Yeah." The throbbing in my ankle was nothing compared with the pressure in my cock.

Pete smiled down at me. "How would you feel about fucking me? I mean, if we could do it in a way that didn't hurt your foot?"

I stared at him. It was a night for experiencing things I hadn't done in a long time. How would I feel about fucking him? Was there more than one way to feel about having a hot guy ask for your dick? "Um, that sounds really great. There are supplies in the bedside table drawer."

But he was already out of bed, rummaging in his jeans. "It's okay. I got it."

Almost instantly he was beside me, his mouth on mine. He trailed kisses across my jaw, down my neck, and whispered, "Lie still. We'll try it this way." He licked across my collarbone and down my chest, his mouth hot as he flicked his tongue across my nipple. I buried my hands in his hair, which felt impossibly soft beneath my fingers.

Pete pulled away. "It'll take me a minute to get ready. It's been a long time."

Rocking onto his heels, he squeezed lube onto the fingers of his right hand. I watched openmouthed as he reached back and began caressing his asshole.

"Turn around so I can see." I couldn't believe I'd said it, but Pete smiled, spun around, and knelt beside me, leaning forward on one hand while with the other he worked fingers into his ass. It was the hottest thing I'd ever seen.

I propped myself on an elbow to watch. I found the half-empty lube pillow and dripped more on the dimple above his ass and on his fingers as they moved in and out of his asshole. I inhaled the smell of ball sweat and musk and ran a finger through the pool of lube. Pete went from two fingers to one, and I slid my index finger next to his. We were almost holding hands as we finger fucked him together.

I pulled my finger out and fumbled for the condom, easing it on with shaking fingers. I was so hard my skin felt stretched. I scooped more lube from where I'd dripped it above Pete's ass. He turned around. I slicked the condom. He bent one leg and straddled me, his breath ragged and his cock a thick, ruddy hook.

Pete held my cock steady and lowered himself onto it, stopping when he'd swallowed the head. He bit his lip, breathing into it. I felt him relax, watched the tension disappear from around his eyes. He took me all the way in, tight and hot and better than I'd imagined. I held his hips and let him fuck himself on me. He started slow, building speed and rocking hard with his eyes closed and head tossed back, the muscles in his legs rippling like wheat in the wind. I held him with one hand to help him balance and used my other to take his cock, stroking him as he rode me, golden, beautiful, breathtaking. His ass started clenching around my cock, and he was coming, long arcs of semen spurting across my belly as I burst through with him, soaring into the searing sun.

* * * *

I heard him rattling around the kitchen. Cupboard doors banged. Water ran. I opened my eyes to a stream of sunlight arrowing across the bed beside me. I closed them again and drifted in a hazy dream that smelled of sex-soaked sheets and coffee.

The bed jostled. This time I opened my eyes to an Adonis, naked except for his farmer's tan, holding two cups of coffee. He thrust one at me with a smile. "Hey, I guessed you like cream since there's a pint of half-and-half in your refrigerator."

I sat, opened my mouth, closed it again, and took the cup.

Pete scowled. "Ah, not your cream."

"Um, sorry."

He nodded and switched cups. "That was my second guess."

I took it gratefully and inhaled the scent of rich, dark coffee. I took a long sip. "Thanks. I can't remember when someone last served me coffee in bed."

"I would have made breakfast, but you're a little short on food. All you have in there is three eggs and half a head of lettuce. But the freezer's full. Do you really live on that crap?"

I shrugged. "Don't knock potpies. Ten bucks a dozen. They make a nice change from ramen."

He gestured around the apartment. "What, you get room, not board?"

I picked at the bedclothes. "It's complicated."

He cocked his head. "And what about your boyfriend? Don't tell me you feed him ramen and potpies."

I shook my head. "He doesn't usually eat here."

Pete contemplated me for a moment and stroked my arm. "Next time I'll bring eggs. What's the use of fucking a farmer if you can't get free food?"

I sipped the coffee. Strong and black, perfect. "Eggs. You keep chickens? I thought you were strictly veggie."

"Nope. Chickens, a pig, bees, a couple of obnoxious goats I'd love to get rid of, and three milk cows, but don't tell the cream drinker. I'm sharing plenty with him already." Pete was making circles with his fingers on my arm. He looked down at me from under pale lashes. "That sounded snide, sorry. I'm a farmer, a little old-fashioned, set in my ways, but I like you. If I have to get more sophisticated and urbane, be cool with the whole open relationship thing in order to see you again, I'm willing to grow up. Last night was…." He cleared his throat. "I had a really good time."

I rested my hand on his thigh. "Yeah, me too. My schedule is, um, unpredictable, I guess, but if you can deal with the possibility of a last-minute cancellation, maybe we could get together again soon. Next Saturday? I'm usually free on weekends."

He gave me a long, thoughtful look. "Good. Now I should re-tape that ankle if you're going to get out of bed anytime soon."

"I can do that." I leaned forward.

Pete shook his head and set my calf over his thigh. "Let me. It'll make me feel useful." He started unwrapping the bandage, his hands a gentle whisper against my skin.

Pete's gaze didn't leave my foot as he rewrapped my ankle. I had to admit he was doing a better job than I ever had.

As he tucked in the bandage end, he looked up. "You know, I met your assemblyman."

I sat straight up, my stomach knotting. "How'd you…. The pictures."

Pete nodded, his hands still cradling my ankle. "That's a good shot of him shaking hands with the governor. And of course, the family portrait." He paused as if waiting for me to say something more. *Deny everything, even if there are pictures.* When I didn't speak, he set my foot on the bed and stood. "I'm on a citizen's committee that met with him about repealing the state's new organic certification law. I don't suppose you'd lobby him to vote to change that law? No, that would be too weird, wouldn't it? Anyway, I thought you should know."

I watched him disappear into the bathroom while my heart banged away in my chest. I closed my eyes and promised God that if Jack and I, and Jack and Pete, and Pete and I, and the whole fucking mess turned out okay, I'd go to Milwaukee for the High Holidays, sit with my mother in Temple, and atone for all my sins.

Pete came out of the bathroom. "Food?"

My cell chirped from the pile of clothing on the bedroom floor. Pete tossed me my pants. I rooted around until I found the phone and answered.

"Hey, Avi." Isaac sounded cheerful. "We're going to the Sunflower for breakfast. You want to meet us there?" I could hear Nathan in the background talking with one of Isaac's many roommates.

I glanced at Pete. "I'm not alone."

"The assemblyman's here on a Sunday morning? What happened to church with the wife and kiddies?"

I cleared my throat. "No, um, you remember I told you about Pete from the market?"

Isaac whooped. "He's there now? Oh, God, now you have to come. Please, please, please?"

I looked at Pete. "We're being invited to breakfast with my friends Isaac and Nathan. Nathan's a nice civilized man, and Isaac is going to be on his best behavior, isn't he?"

"Of course not." Isaac laughed.

"Sure." Pete smiled. "I'm starving."

I turned my attention back to the phone. "I'm going to regret this. See you there."

* * * *

Jack had a thing about his teeth. He kept a stack of unopened toothbrushes in the medicine cabinet. I handed one to Pete and lent him my razor. And made the mistake of joining him in the shower. Which meant we were slow getting out of the apartment. After all, we had to re-tape my ankle. The Sunflower was only two blocks from the apartment—an easy walk, even on crutches.

Nutrient pollution was a problem for Madison-area lakes. Lake Monona always smelled green—in August it was like rotting compost—but in June the lake smelled like mowed grass. A gentle breeze stirred the air, and between buildings we could catch glimpses of the sun sparkling on the waves.

Pete strolled beside me, matching my lurching pace. "Is this part of your routine? Introducing your Saturday night conquests to your pals?"

I glanced at him. His gaze was focused on the sidewalk. He thought I did this a lot? "Nope. This is a first."

He glanced up. "Will they think it's weird you're not with what's his face?"

I shook my head. "They've never met him."

Pete stared at me. "Never?"

I kept going, swinging my body between the crutches. "It's not that kind of relationship, Pete. Please don't bring it up."

He strode past me and opened the door. "Gotcha."

The café—a classic hippie joint with mismatched furniture—smelled of cinnamon and coffee, and served omelets with sprouts on the side and some of the best baked goods in town. Indie folk played as soft background music for dozens of conversations.

And there, at the first table by the door, sat Prof Joan, having breakfast with her husband, a wiry, blond artist I'd met several times at history department functions. A couple of times a year some event brought the faculty and graduate students together, along with their significant others and even sometimes their children. I always showed up alone.

"Good morning, Avi." She gestured to her husband. "You remember Jerry." Her gaze slid to Pete.

I swallowed. It didn't get more public than this. I glanced at Pete. He stood beside me with that beautiful smile. I introduced him, standing a little taller in my crutches. After all, anyone would be proud to claim him. The four of us chatted for a moment, Jerry asking about my ankle. Prof Joan said Pete looked familiar, and Pete replied that he'd probably sold her a tomato. As we stepped away from their table, I shook my head in amazement. The whole encounter had felt comfortable and normal and completely different from my life as I knew it.

Isaac and Nathan had taken a table in the back. I paused to watch them for a moment. Nathan sat angled toward Isaac, who was speaking animatedly, his hands flying like birds as he described something to Nathan. They weren't touching, but something about the nonchalance of Nathan's hand on the back of Isaac's chair and the gentleness of Nathan's gaze was almost more intimate than a kiss.

With a jolt, I realized that Nathan was wearing a polo shirt exactly like one in Jack's closet—blue cotton mesh with three shiny white buttons at the collar, an unmistakably middle-aged style. And yet, despite their similar coloring and

Nathan's occasional joking fear that someone would mistake him for Isaac's father, Nathan and Isaac looked happy and settled, and anyone who saw them would know they were in love.

Isaac spotted me and waved. I led Pete through the crowded café. On crutches, I negotiated the small spaces between tables with some difficulty. By the time I got to the table, I was grateful to prop my crutches against the wall and fall into the seat across from Isaac.

"Isaac Wolf, Nathan Kohn—this is Pete Jakobsen." I gestured as he sat beside me, the odd man out, a muscular Dane in the company of skinny Jews.

Everyone shook hands, and I ignored the look Isaac shot me. Yes, I knew sleeping with Pete could endanger my relationship with Jack, and no, I didn't want to look at why that seemed like an okay idea. The waitress brought menus and coffee, and I stuck my head in one while drinking the other.

"Isaac says you have a stall at the farmers' market?" Nathan asked as soon as she'd taken our orders and strolled off. "You grow the stuff you sell?" Pete nodded, and Nathan continued. "How'd you get into farming?"

Pete shrugged. "I grew up on the farm. I guess sometimes you end up where you started. My father died while I was in graduate school in California at UC Davis. He left the farm to my sister and me. I took the semester off to come back and help her sell the land to some developer to divide into McMansion-sized parcels."

Pete paused. I looked at him. He'd been to graduate school? Who knew?

Isaac shook his head. "Another fucking academic. This city is crawling with them. You came back, fell in love with the land, and had to stay?"

Pete laughed. "Not quite. The market tanked, the land didn't sell, and we had to come up with a way to feed ourselves. It was a few years before I fell in love with the place, but now I'd do just about anything to keep from having to sell. Farming's hard work, and we're always broke, but the land sinks into your bones."

Conversation stopped as the waitress delivered plates heaped with eggs, potatoes and thick slabs of toast. I inhaled deeply, and my stomach grumbled. Pete smiled at me, probably thinking about how I'd worked up my appetite.

Nathan took a bite of blueberry muffin and groaned. He broke off a piece and held it in front Isaac. "Oh honey, you have to try this. You'll like it. I promise."

Isaac held Nathan's gaze as he took the muffin, licking Nathan's fingers in the process. I watched Nathan's Adam's apple bounce as he stared at Isaac's mouth around his fingers. He might be the same age, wear the same clothes, and even use the same phrases as Jack, but when he looked at Isaac, it was clear that Nathan and Jack had nothing in common.

Pete chewed a mouthful of egg and cheese and asked Nathan and Isaac, "What do you guys do?"

Nathan wrenched his attention away from Isaac. "Isaac has one more year of school to become an environmental engineer, and I'm in transition. There's an excellent aquatics lab here at the university, and they've given me bench space for the summer. After that, I'll finish up one more year at Saint Genevieve's College and then...." He glanced at Isaac. "Who knows?"

Isaac pushed eggs around his plate with a fork. "He's giving up a successful career so that I can get a fresh start. It's an incredible gift."

Nathan's gaze was soft on Isaac. "Some things are more important. And nearly twenty years is a long time to do one thing. It's time for a change." He turned to Pete. "Maybe in California. I have a friend there who's scouting jobs for us."

Pete looked from Nathan to Isaac, his face unreadable. "That's the problem with academics, isn't it? The jobs are scarce, and you need to move to find one. But California's a great place to live. You'll like the weather. Nothing like Wisconsin winters to make you appreciate the sun."

I looked at Isaac, who was staring thoughtfully at his plate, and thought about big love, big trust, and all the sacrifices they entailed.

* * * *

Pete walked me home from breakfast. The air was thick and warm—it was like walking through my grandmother's chicken soup. The space between us seemed bigger than before breakfast. It had been a while since I'd let the circles of my life intersect. I didn't know how to be with Pete after he'd met my friends.

I cleared my throat. "You raise pigs?"

Pete smiled, and I breathed easier with him. "Oh. You're Jewish, right? Are you religious?"

I shook my head. "I go to my mom's for holidays, but that's about it. But I was raised very observant. I'm pretty sure I'd choke on pork."

He looked at me. "We only have the one hog that Logan's raising for 4–H. He plans to sell it in the fall. Suits me. It's a pain in the ass—the damned thing's always trying to escape. So you'll be safe from pigs out at the farm soon enough."

And suddenly the void between us was back as I contemplated a normal life where I could visit Pete at the farm and Pete thought about whatever it was he was thinking. Which was what, exactly? I hardly knew him at all.

Pete broke the silence as we neared the apartment. "Nathan seems like a stable guy. Good thing. Your Isaac's got the look of a lost boy about him. Had some rough times, that one has."

I glanced at him. "You got all that from breakfast?"

He shrugged. "They're nice. I'm glad we went." We neared my doorway, and he stopped. "Now I should get home. Make sure Logan got everything done."

Great, he was already bored. I looked at his feet, thinking that scuffed boots had a kind of sexiness I hadn't noticed before. "Yeah, sure. Thanks."

He touched my arm. I looked up. He smiled. "I'd come up to say good-bye properly, but the chores would never get done."

I nodded.

His eyes in the daylight sparkled a lighter blue. "Next Saturday is a long way away."

I grimaced. "I can't plan ahead, Pete."

"Yeah, I know."

My phone sounded with Jack's ring. I jumped. "Um, I have to get this."

"Sure. Of course. Call me." Striding away, he called, "And come by the stall on Wednesday. I'll feed you."

I watched until he turned the corner before answering the phone. "Hi."

"Took you long enough." Jack's voice radiated irritation.

"Sorry, I couldn't find the phone." I leaned on my crutches, holding the phone awkwardly against my ear. "Are you coming down?"

"Can you believe it? Richardson called a Sunday night dinner meeting. The man has no heart." His voice dropped to a whisper. "I tried to talk her out of it, but Peggy insisted on leaving the boys with her mother and coming with me."

I blinked into the sun. "Oh, when will you get here?"

He sighed. "We leave in an hour and should be there by five. Maybe it's best if you clear out for the week." With a nervous laugh, he signed off.

I limped into the apartment lobby and hit the elevator button, hoping I had time to wash the sheets.

Chapter Seven

The apartment was scrubbed clean of any traces of Pete, me, and male sexual activity in general. I'd even aired the place out and emptied the garbage on the off chance Jack or Peggy noticed the used rubbers or Pete's toothbrush in the trash. I dumped the bedside table supplies into a shoe box, noting, as usual, the irony as I crammed everything onto the top shelf of the closet in the boys' bedroom.

I filled my backpack with all the crap I'd need for a week away and topped it off with my research papers. Isaac's house was near campus, and I planned to spend the week in the library working on the damned Project due now in what… nine weeks? I slung the pack over my shoulders, slid my laptop into my messenger bag, and glanced around the apartment to make sure I hadn't missed anything. Peggy knew I was the caretaker. It's not like I had to completely erase myself, but it always seemed like a good idea to keep my footprint small.

The pack was heavy, and the bag banged against my crutches with every step. I felt like a soldier returning from the Revolutionary War, bandaged and limping, with all my worldly goods on my back. It was good to wallow in self-pity every now and then—kept me honest.

Isaac lived in classic student squalor with seven other guys in an old five-bedroom house in the Vilas district. He and Nathan probably could have sublet Isaac's room and gotten a real apartment for the summer, but Nathan was still paying rent on his place in Chicago, and they were saving up for the big move to California in the spring. I didn't think they minded being crammed together in Isaac's tiny room for the summer, since winters were long with a lover hours away.

It wasn't uncommon for me to crash on Isaac's disgusting basement couch when Jack's family was in town. Even if I'd wanted to stay long term, every room was rented out. But the house was so full of people coming and going that Isaac's roommates barely acknowledged I was there. The house had been student digs since the sixties. It was drafty in the winter, loud on weekends, and the landlord was hands-off to the point of negligence, but the rent was cheap and the forced camaraderie so good that nostalgia pulled the odd alumnus back for weekends. One such recent graduate had donated a lumpy hideaway sofa to make a guest room out of the unfinished basement. It had its share of use during the year when weekend parties produced hookups of various gender combinations in need of a soft spot to lie.

I shoved a few dollars in the beer money jar to cover my rent, hobbled downstairs, dumped my gear in a corner, and slumped onto the couch to rest. I closed my eyes, and my mind filled with the image of Pete's face, close enough that I could make out the pale skin in the creases of the fine lines around his eyes. I realized I wasn't even a little bit sorry that I couldn't see Jack this week. Which was a fucking awkwardness I didn't want to think about since I really did need a place to live.

* * * *

It wasn't until Wednesday morning, sitting at the table I'd snagged near an outlet at my favorite neighborhood coffee shop, that I realized I'd left a folder of critical papers back at the apartment. I stared at my computer screen for about an hour, trying to figure out how to finish drafting the chapter without them. The coffeehouse smelled of fresh baked goods and dark roast. I toyed with the idea of blowing off the rest of the week.

But if I didn't get the draft done by August, I'd be out of choices. I loaded my work into my messenger bag, grabbed the crutches, and hobbled out to suck in the hot, humid air and catch a bus up the hill.

The apartment building seemed to shimmer in the heat. As the bus fumes dissipated, I could smell the lake. I unlocked the front door and pushed into the cool, dry lobby, hoping Peggy had things of her own to do on a warm summer day. Coming out of the elevator, I almost turned around when I heard the music—some variation of country, judging by the beat. We'd met a couple of times in the first year. She was lovely in a petite, blonde sort of way, charming and gracious. I felt like an ass for sleeping with her husband, so I'd avoided her ever since. But she didn't know. How could she? I knocked.

On the other side of the door, the music quieted.

I called out. "It's me, Avi Rosen, Mrs. Krausman. The caretaker?"

I heard her undo the door chain. There was silence.

"Mrs. Krausman? I'm sorry to disturb you, but I need to pick something up."

The knob turned, and the door opened a crack. "Are you alone?"

I looked up and down the hallway. It was empty, like always. "Um. Yes, ma'am."

"You might as well come in." She sighed and pulled the door all the way open. I stepped in, feeling oddly displaced in my home. I turned to greet her and stopped, shocked by the bruising on her neck. I felt suddenly dizzy and cold.

"Jack." I stared at the imprint of his fingers on her pale skin.

She shrugged. "You know how he gets."

I opened my mouth and closed it. Scenarios tumbled through my mind as I tried to decide if I was seeing the aftermath of sex play or attempted murder. And where were the boundaries for a conversation with someone when you were sleeping with her husband?

I reached for my wallet. "Um, should you see someone? I mean like a doctor? I have the card of a woman whose office is near here."

"Wouldn't that be a fun scandal?" She rested her hand on her hip and looked at me. "I'm fine. And we're used to it, aren't we? He does a lot of things he shouldn't, doesn't he?"

My stomach clenched. How long had she known? I couldn't hold her gaze.

She touched her neck with one slim hand, and her wedding ring caught the light. "I hope it goes away by the weekend. This isn't exactly turtleneck weather, and I can't make my mother keep the boys forever." She gestured toward my foot. "Looks like you have your own war stories."

I sputtered, "It's not…. It was a bike accident."

"Uh-huh, and I walked into a door." She turned toward the kitchen. "You want a cup of coffee?"

"No, I couldn't—"

She fluttered her hand dismissively. "Of course you could. I haven't talked face-to-face with anyone but Jack in days, and I'm going crazy. It's the least you can do, don't you think?"

I followed her into the kitchen and accepted the coffee. A giant bunch of roses dominated the table. Peggy glanced at them. "According to the card, he's sorry."

She sank into a chair across from me. When I'd seen her before, Peggy had been put together well. Now she looked young and vulnerable sitting with her arms resting on the kitchen table, dressed in shorts and one of Jack's tees with no makeup and lank hair, those bruises her only decoration. It was overwhelmingly sad.

"I'd offer you cake, but I finished the last piece an hour ago. I'm going to have to spend next week on the grapefruit diet."

I watched steam rise from my coffee cup. "It's fine. I'm not hungry."

We sipped in silence for a moment. I couldn't think of anything to say. I'd spent years trying not to think about Peggy or telling myself she'd never know. And here we were sipping coffee together at the kitchen table where I'd blown Jack only days before. My chest tightened with guilt.

"I don't blame you, you know." I looked up to see her watching me. "If it wasn't you, it would be someone else. There probably is already, some man neither of us knows anything about. Someone in his campaign office, probably. He likes to have them on payroll. That's our Jack, always in control. I don't think he has other women, but I could be fooling myself. I'm good at that. You don't happen to have a cigarette, do you?"

Peggy Krausman was one tough lady. If I'd been in her shoes, I was pretty sure I'd be throwing them. Jack didn't deserve her. I shook my head. "I don't smoke."

She drummed her fingers on the tabletop. "Jack thinks I quit, and I only smoke when he's down here. But right now, I feel trapped."

I cleared my throat. "I could take you somewhere, if you like."

She shook her head. "Our lives are constrained by reporters and the threat of scandal. Even if I didn't care what happened to Jack, my boys need a daddy they can look up to."

That wasn't a good enough excuse for putting up with Jack, not if he hurt her and not if she knew about...about me. Sure, boys needed wonderful fathers. But not every boy got one. And yet we survived. I started to speak, but she held up her hand.

"Even if he isn't the man they believe he is." She patted my arm. "We're all good at keeping his secrets. Let's stay that way."

I focused on my arm where she'd touched me.

"I'm sorry." It came out unexpectedly hoarse.

"I know. I forgive you. We're all doing what we need to, to get by." She leaned toward the roses and inhaled. "I even forgive him. Though God knows why."

I stared at those bruises on her neck, wondering how I'd forgive either one of us. When I left she was still sitting at the table, staring out the window at the Capitol.

* * * *

I'd told Pete I'd stop by. The whole encounter with Peggy left me feeling shaky. I wasn't up for conversation, so I was grateful to see his stall was busy. I gave his hand a quick squeeze, but didn't stay to talk and insisted on paying him for the berries I bought. At another booth I picked up handmade chocolate truffles. I stopped for cigarettes on the way back to the apartment, choosing the most elegant-looking brand I could see. I hung a bag filled with cigarettes, chocolate and strawberries on the doorknob, knocked, and called out. As I heard her steps near, I loped back toward the elevator as quickly as my crutches could take me. I knew I was being a coward, but I didn't want to face her, or those angry marks again. Peggy deserved better from Jack. And from me.

* * * *

Jack called Friday afternoon to let me know he and Peggy were leaving the next morning and that I could have the apartment back around noon. As he spoke, I had an image of the bruises fading slowly from her neck. I wanted to ask him what the fuck he thought he was doing strangling his wife, but swallowed hard and reminded myself that I was always a few wrong words away from homeless.

I talked Isaac into taking me along for Nathan's Friday night, after-work Rathskeller party. It felt good to be in the company of smart, happy people and multicolored pitchers of beer.

Chapter Eight

I woke with a pounding headache, barely remembering the evening after we'd left the Rathskeller. Had I really ridden to dinner on the back of Callie's motorcycle? I looked around the bedroom, my crutches leaning against the wall by my bed, and I had a fleeting vision of doing whiskey shots at some State Street dive and of being crammed in the back of a cab beside Isaac and Nathan. They must have brought me home and put me to bed. Good to have friends.

I glanced at my watch. Only five hours before I was supposed to be tantalizing company for Pete. With a groan, I crawled out of bed. I tried some weight on my foot. It held. Amazingly, no damage from debauchery. I limped to the kitchen to make coffee.

Two cups later, after a shower and shave, and tired of doing the alphabet over and over, I spelled out the preamble to the Declaration of Independence with my foot. According to the Internet, two weeks put me about halfway through my crutch-needing time.

It had rained during the night. I sat at the kitchen table, watched the sun sparkle off the Capitol dome, drank another cup of coffee, and finished the *New York Times*. I checked my watch. *It's ten in the morning. Do you know where your lovers are?* I contemplated Jack's image in a family photo and imagined him hiking through the woods with his son. Deer frolicked in meadows, fish jumped in lakes, and wolves howled in the distance. It's how I always saw him when he was at home in Eagle River—a place I'd never been, somewhere in the wilds of the north woods. That image seemed more sinister now that I'd seen Peggy's damaged neck. Pete, on the other hand, I could easily picture, only a few blocks away in his blue T-shirt and rainbow bandana, standing behind piles of green vegetables, laughing with everyone who came along. Wholesome, honest, a great guy. I didn't understand how he was still single or why he was willing to put up with my sordid life.

I stared at the phone for a few minutes. And dialed.

"Hey, gorgeous." Pete's voice poured into me like warm honey. "Don't tell me you're calling to cancel. I mean, I'm cool with it of course, but—"

"It's okay." I stopped him. "We're on for tonight. I wanted to know when."

"Just a sec." I heard a clatter as he must have put down the phone, followed by a lengthy discussion about the Wisconsin growing season and when some woman with a shrill voice could expect tomatoes. He came back. "Sorry about that. Logan, take over for a minute, would ya? Thanks."

"I'm sorry. I shouldn't have called you at work. I wasn't thinking."

"No." His breath came out in a rush. "It's fine. What are your plans this afternoon?"

I glanced at my book bag, which lay slumped against a chair. "Working on The Project."

"What project?"

"Oh, um, my dissertation. It needs to be done by the end of the summer. But if you've got something better in mind, bring it on. I'm sick to death of the thing."

Pete laughed. "I get that. Well, if you're really willing to ditch it for the afternoon, Brynne's having coffee with an old friend tomorrow morning, and she offered to drop me off after we're done here and pick me up around noon tomorrow. Would that work for you?"

My heart and mind raced. Jack never missed the opportunity to go to church with his constituents back home. Which meant that unless he called at the last minute wanting to spend Saturday night with me—something that hadn't happened in the two years I'd been seeing him—there was no way their paths would intersect. I didn't want to think about what would happen if I was wrong.

"Great. I'll see you when? About two?"

"Better make it two thirty. I want to help Brynne and Logan load the truck and take whatever's left to the food pantry. After that, I'll have her swing by and let me off."

"Okay, see you then." There was a pause. Was I expected to say something else?

Pete whispered, "I'm looking forward to it." And the line went dead.

I sat staring out the window at the Capitol, wondering when I had gotten too cool to say something like that. Was it before or after I started seeing Jack? Back then, I was twenty-eight and drunk with my own possibilities. Now, approaching thirty, I sat at Jack's kitchen table, watching the traffic circle Jack's workplace, jaded, discouraged and still only a couple of chapters into the damned Project. I poured out the rest of my coffee and started sorting my papers into piles on the table, hoping to redeem myself with work.

At two, I took down the box of supplies and transferred condoms and lube to the bedside table. At two twenty-three, the buzzer rang. Pete's voice sounded tinny through the little speaker. I buzzed him up and hobbled to open the door.

He burst into the apartment, a crate filled with produce under one arm and an overnight bag in the other.

I eyed the box. Lush greens overflowed the edges like a bouquet. "You brought food?"

"I don't like ramen." He shifted the box to his hip. "Let me put this in the kitchen. It's heavier than it looks."

It looked heavy enough. I gestured toward the kitchen and followed him through.

Pete set the box on the counter and turned to me with a slow grin. "I don't think I greeted you properly."

He stepped close. His hands were gentle as he tipped my chin up and brought his mouth to mine. He smelled of sunshine and green growing things. I rested my hands on his hips. His kiss reminded me of the first strawberry in spring, sweet and finished far too soon. He rubbed his thumb across my jaw and held my gaze with eyes the color of dusk in the summer sky.

"Hey, heartbreaker. Are you hungry?"

I reared back. "Heartbreaker?"

He nodded. "Yep, I'm pretty sure that's you. And when was the last time you ate?"

I looked around the kitchen, trying to remember. "I had cereal this morning."

He pressed me into a chair, hauled another one over and propped up my foot. "Well, I'm starving. I might as well feed you."

"I can help." I started to stand, but he waved me down.

"You'll only get in the way. Besides, the sooner your foot gets better, the sooner I can put those crutches back in that dusty loft where they belong." He started unloading things from the box, keeping up a running commentary as he went. "I got this bread from Lisa who runs the bakery stall on the corner. You know the one with cinnamon buns? I love it, and she always runs out. I traded her eggs for bread first thing this morning. The cheese is a goat cheddar. That okay with you?"

I shrugged my assent. What did I know? I was the guy who lived on cheap potpies.

He continued. "Good. Now all I need is a knife, a cutting board, and a frying pan. I would have brought my own, but I figured you had to have at least those three things."

I pointed to the appropriate cupboards. He found what he needed, and I watched him dice onions and mushrooms and toss them into the pan. "Why is a guy like you single?"

He raised his eyebrows. "That's the nicest thing you've ever said to me."

I rolled my eyes. "No, I mean really."

"You're honestly the first single..." He frowned. "Make that available gay and attractive guy I've been around since I moved back."

"There's that lowered bar again."

He grinned. "I did say that attractive was a major criteria and my standards are high."

Good to know I passed. "What about before that? Did you leave someone behind in California?"

He focused on the pan, stirring the onions and mushrooms. When he spoke, his voice was soft. "There was someone. His name was Rick. We lived together. But he was a compulsive gambler. A month before my dad died, Rick emptied our bank account and left. I sat in our house with the shades drawn. Then my dad died, and it sounded like a good idea to pack up and come out here to take care of Brynne and Logan."

"Oh, shit. I'm sorry." What was it about money that always complicated relationships?

He shook it off. "Thank you. It's been years. I'm over it now." He cut big slabs of bread, covered them with butter, cheese and the sauté mix, browned them up, and delivered the best-looking grilled cheese I'd ever seen.

I inhaled the smell of toasted bread and cheese. "Where'd you learn to cook like this?"

He smiled and pulled two wheat beers from the fridge. "Rick was a chef. I picked up a few things." He handed me a beer. "It's good for impressing dates."

I took a bite of my sandwich. Warm cheese oozed out the sides. My taste buds stood up and applauded. "Consider me impressed."

He dropped into the chair across from me. "Good."

"What do you want to do this afternoon?" I tossed Pete a napkin and got another to wipe the grease dripping down my chin.

"Oh, I'm sure we'll think of something." He winked, and my cock came to attention.

I washed down a last bite of sandwich with beer. "Eat up. I'll do the dishes."

Pete grinned. "Good man." He handed me his plate.

* * * *

The bedroom was dark after the bright kitchen light. Pete's mouth tasted of beer and cheese, and our lips slithered together in greased desire. I let him push me back on the bed, his tongue in my mouth a welcome invader. For the first time, my ankle didn't throb as I moved against him, and I relished the release, the ability to focus on his skin sleek beneath my hands, the ripple of his muscles, his hot breath. Pete was granite hard, and his excitement infected me. I wrapped my legs around him, our cocks rubbing together like a second kiss.

Pete's hands glided down my back and cupped my ass.

"I had a dream about you." His breath against my ear sent jolts of want straight to my groin.

I slipped my hands into his hair and pulled him up so I could look into his eyes. "What did you dream?"

His irises had almost disappeared around his dilated pupils. He gripped my ass and slid his dick in a long, slow stroke against mine. "We were on a blanket in the barn. I remember the smell of fresh hay. You were tight around me and really hot."

I groaned, captured by the image and by the heat in his eyes. I gestured with my head to the restocked bedside table and unwrapped my legs so he could move. "Condoms and lube in the top drawer."

I barely registered the cool of my skin with him gone, and he was back, this time with his hand making gentle circles on my balls. I spread my legs wide, and Pete sat on his heels with his thighs tucked under mine. He dribbled lube onto the hand he moved slowly along my perineum and made searing orbits around the pucker of my ass. I grabbed my knees to give him more access, and a finger slipped in with a burn. Another entered me, and I pressed back at him, wanting more.

"Jesus," Pete whispered. He tossed me a condom. His fingers shifting deeper into me as I tore open the packet. Pete's breath rushed out in a long gasp as I rolled the condom on him and drizzled him with lube. Pete slipped his fingers out. I felt the tip of his cock against my ass and wrapped my legs over his shoulders. Our gaze locked, and he pushed in, pausing with every inch to let me settle around him. My ass blazed with need, and I shoved myself over him, impatient for the full feel of him.

"Oh, God." It sounded like a prayer. I clawed at his back, and Pete plunged into me. I thrust back, wanting everything he was giving, the space between us on fire. Sweat pearled and ran down his chest and arms, dripping tiny warm pools on my skin. I grabbed the headboard so I could push back even harder. Pete's balls slapped against my ass, and our twinned breaths came in short rasps. His eyes flashed, and he reached between us, his fingers still slick with lube, and stroked my cock in the same rhythm he was pounding into me. My skin felt as flushed as Pete's. I held on tight as my orgasm washed through like a rainstorm, wetting both our bellies, and Pete came crashing after me. We lay sweaty and semen drenched in the afternoon heat.

* * * *

I must have dozed off. I opened my eyes to Pete's smile. He lay with his head propped on an elbow, the sheets bunched beneath his arm. He watched me, his eyes like marbles half-hidden by his lids. His hair curled around his face like another form of sunshine. He skimmed his fingers across my belly, up to tangle in the hair on my chest. I reached for him, and he folded into my kiss. He pulled away, and I realized that the air had shifted between us. We had each taken and been taken, and I could feel the difference. Pete caressed my jaw. I breathed him in.

And my phone buzzed.

Pete looked at me and walked to the bathroom. I fumbled in the pocket of my jeans, which lay crumpled on the floor, found the damned thing, and answered.

"Hi, baby," Jack grumbled in my ear.

"Um, hi." I stood, grabbed one crutch, and limped into the living room, aware of Pete within earshot. I wasn't usually the one in need of discretion.

He continued. "I've only got a minute. I'm waiting for Peggy and the kids to come out of a store, but I wanted to tell you I won't be down tomorrow. We're having a big campaign meeting up here on Monday, and I won't make it to Madison until Wednesday at the earliest."

The afternoon light turned the buildings a beautiful rose gold. Relief wound its guilty way through me as I stared out the window, trying to puzzle out why he was giving me this much notice. I had a paranoid instant thinking he knew about Pete and it was all a trick. But that was ridiculous on a number of levels. He seemed to be waiting for a response.

"Okay. I'll be here." It was the best I could do at the moment.

It must have pleased him, because he gave a dirty-old-man chuckle. "I know you will. I'm looking forward to playing with our new toy again." The line went dead.

Lights went on around the Capitol dome.

"This is a hell of a view." Pete rubbed my arms, his chest pressed against my back. "How was your phone call?"

I shrugged.

He rested his chin against my head. "Is the assemblyman coming down tonight?"

I turned to look at him. He looked back, his face blank but his eyes still warm.

I stepped away from him and limped toward the refrigerator. "I guess it wasn't hard to figure out the identity of my secret benefactor. I wouldn't have made a very good spy, would I?"

He shook his head. "You'd be terrible at clandestine work." He accepted a beer from me and sank onto a chair, resting his elbows on the table, his legs spread akimbo.

"Thanks." I took the chair across from him, propping my foot on the third. They were the exact positions we'd taken at lunch, only then we'd been clothed.

He smiled at me. "The inability to deceive is not a bad trait in a lover."

"Terrible one in a mistress." The beer tasted hoppy and cold. "You can't tell anyone. Promise?"

He smirked. "I'm not in the business of ruining lives. I leave that to the politicians."

"Very funny."

Pete leaned forward. He stroked the yellow trace of a bruise on my wrist. "You're also not good at hiding these. Is this his handiwork?"

I yanked my hand away from his and looked at the pale residue of the bruise. "It's fine."

Pete sat back, his arms folded across his chest. "Is that what you like? Do you want me to tie you up?"

"No." It came out too quickly and too loud.

He nodded. "Nice guy, your assemblyman."

"Drop it," I snapped. "I don't want to talk about it."

He contemplated me for a moment. "Right. Still working on the whole open relationship thing. I keep forgetting what you do with him isn't my business. You got an apron?"

I blinked, confused but grateful for the subject change. "An apron?"

He gestured to his privates, which rested like a sleeping animal on the seat between his legs. "I don't want to injure myself while I'm making your fabulous dinner."

I pointed toward a kitchen drawer. "Peggy keeps a few down there."

His eyebrows rose, but he didn't say anything. He strolled to the drawer in question and produced a full-length pink apron with large black letters spelling out THIS KITCHEN IS SEASONED WITH LOVE.

I shook my head, fighting an irony attack. He looped the apron around his neck and tied it in back. Naked except for the apron had to be someone's fantasy. I had a feeling that from now on it might be mine.

* * * *

"Come to the farm with me tomorrow."

We lay sweat drenched amid tangled sheets, my head cradled on Pete's shoulder.

He stroked my hair. "My sister and nephew will be there, so we can't run around naked, shagging each other in the fields, but I'd like to show it to you."

I shook my head. "I should work on The Project."

"Bring your stuff. You work while I milk cows and feed chickens." He jostled my head. "Come on. It'll be fun. I'll bring you back Monday after chores."

He smiled down at me with those beautiful teeth. How could I say no? Besides, Jack wasn't coming back until Wednesday.

"Okay." I nestled closer and promptly fell asleep.

Chapter Nine

The ride out to the farm could have been more comfortable if we weren't trying to fit three adults on the bench seat of an old pickup. Pete drove, I took the middle seat, straddling the stick shift, and Brynne slumped against the door, peppering me with questions about my childhood, my relationship history, and my employment plans.

Eventually Pete said, "Enough, Brynne. He can show you his W-2s another day."

I snorted. "Yeah, because that will impress you."

She leaned forward and addressed her brother. "I'm trying to get to know the man. Leave me alone."

"You're grilling him. See if you can put on your secret warrior cape and pretend you have social skills."

"You're an asshole."

"But you love me."

Longest twenty minutes of my life.

Finally we turned onto a gravel road beside a large sign advertising JAKOBSEN'S FARMS. On one side stretched a cultivated field with long rows of plants separated by dirt trenches. Clover covered the field on the other side. We bumped down the road, dust billowing behind us, and pulled up beside an old white farmhouse. A huge barn loomed behind the house. Beyond that sat three long hoop greenhouses.

Pete killed the engine and turned to me. "Home sweet home."

Brynne cracked open her door, letting in the smell of dirt and hay. She climbed out and headed toward the barn, where Logan stood flanked by two large dogs. I started to get out, but Pete grabbed my arm.

He brought his lips to my ear. "Don't mind her. She's being big-sister protective."

I closed my eyes, savoring his breath on my neck. "Don't worry about it. Wait until you meet my mom."

He whispered, "I look forward to it."

Did I just invite him to meet my mother? He handed me my crutches. I slid out of the truck and followed Pete into the house in a daze.

I expected the old farmhouse to be decorated one of two ways—either with doilies and worn slipcovers or in a hippie kaleidoscope of East Indian prints. Given the whole organic farm thing, my expectations were leaning toward the latter. Instead I walked into a beautifully restored home with polished floors, antiques, and tasteful watercolors dotting the walls.

"This is gorgeous," I whispered.

"It is, isn't it? My mom was into decorating, and Brynne has kept it up. Those are Brynne's watercolors." Pete smiled. That was gorgeous too. He led me through the living room to a sun porch that looked over a meadow, complete with grazing cows. He gestured out the window. "We're into crop rotation. This is this year's view. Next year it'll be the veggies."

I tried to picture next year's view. With any luck, by then I'd have a job somewhere far away. The thought made me unreasonably sad.

Pete continued, "You might think those are milk cows, and you'd be right, but I see them as fertilizer factories."

I made a face. "I'll try not to think of that the next time I drink milk."

Pete laughed. "There are chickens running around out there also. You might as well think of it with your eggs too."

I peered at the field, trying to spot a chicken. "Don't chickens need coops?"

"See that blue wooden trailer with windows? That's the egg mobile. On this farm, free-range means we bring the coop to the chicken, not the chicken to the coop." He stacked papers and closed a laptop to clear a space on a desk overlooking the field. "You go ahead and set up. I've got to help Brynne and Logan."

"What are you going to do?"

He pointed out the window. "Do you see that fence?"

I noticed a line of fence posts running through the grass, which was noticeably higher on the far side of the fence.

"Except for the apple orchard, we have the whole farm, about forty acres, fenced off in five-acre chunks. We always have two of those in vegetable production and the others in some sort of forage. Every Sunday during the growing season, we move the cows to the next section." He pointed to Logan, who was walking toward the field, a yellow dog on one side and a black-and-white one on the other. "You'll want to watch Logan work the dogs. I keep thinking we should put it online."

It looked like a lot of work to me.

Pete sighed. "My dad, God rest his soul, worked the soil pretty hard. We're still rebuilding it. Besides, the way we farm, ten acres is plenty to have in intensive cultivation. We share a crew of a dozen temporary workers with a farm down the road, but even so, we're at our limit. We're in a Catch-22. We farm organically, but can't afford certification and so can't charge that kind of premium. As it is, we're always at the edge, a bill or two away from having to let the place go. If that damned certification law doesn't get repealed, who knows how long we'll last." He paused, chewing his lip. He shook his head. "Look at me, babbling away. I promised you that you could work here. I'll get out of your way." He leaned in and kissed my forehead. "Make yourself at home."

"Have fun," I called after him as he strode from the room.

I looked around the sun porch, the only furniture the desk, chair, and a comfortable-looking armchair with a lamp looming over it and piles of books beside. This was Pete's space. I could feel it. The stacks of paper and books had his nonchalance and the deep red, braided rug his warmth. I plugged in my laptop, sat down in his chair, and felt a calm descend. Maybe I could finish Chapter Two after all.

When I looked up, I saw Pete walking open a huge swinging gate. Logan and Brynne were hooking up an ATV to the egg mobile. Brynne pulled the trailer through the gate, followed by a line of cows. Logan stood in the middle of the field. I could hear muffled shouts and whistles. His dogs ran in wide loops through the grass. Eventually a line of chickens converged, strutting through the gate behind the cows. Logan sent the dogs on a couple of final circuits around the field before strolling through and shutting the gate. Pete was right. They should get it on film.

* * * *

Dinner at the farm was a group production. After feeding his dogs and settling them on a bed in the corner, Logan filled a sink with water and began methodically washing a basket of greens.

I nodded toward the dogs, who lay curled together. "I saw your show earlier. How did you teach them to do that?"

Logan lit up. "They're great, aren't they? I got a DVD on training dogs to herd sheep. Lady got it right away. We think she's part heeler." The black-and-white dog lifted her muzzle and looked at him. The other dog looked up too when he continued, "Homer took longer to get the hang of it. But I think he's got it now."

"And we only lost one chicken in the process." Pete patted Logan's back and set a pile of carrots on the long butcher-block table that dominated the center of the kitchen. Pete gestured to a stool and handed me a peeler.

"That's not fair." The dogs watched Logan as he spoke. "That chicken dropped dead on her own. Homer just brought her in."

Pete smiled and cracked eggs into a big bowl. Brynne stood next to me chopping onions. When the prep work was complete, Pete cooked, Logan tossed a salad, and Brynne scrubbed down the table and set it with place mats, knives, forks, and napkins. The kitchen filled with the smell of cooking butter, onions and cheese. My stomach started to rumble. She dropped two huge chunks of cheese in the middle of the table and began sawing thick slices of bread from a round loaf.

She saw me watching. "When I was sixteen, I spent a year in France as part of a student exchange program. The family I lived with had a table like this where they prepared and ate dinner. I whined so much when I got home that Dad made this for me. We've been eating on it ever since."

"It's great. Very European."

"Mama always said an elegant setting enhances simple food." Brynne poured milk for Logan and handed beers around for the adults.

Logan rolled his eyes at his mother and placed his salad on the table. "I thought you told me she ran off with some guy. Was the whole elegant table thing before or after that?"

Pete shrugged. "Must have been before, eh, sport? Not like she's said much to us since then."

I stared at him. "Your mother is still alive? I guess I assumed she died before your dad."

Pete pulled a pan from the oven and transferred wedges of frittata onto four plates. Cheese dripped from each wedge to pool on the plate beneath. "She might as well have. Left without a backward glance when we were in high school."

Brynne passed me a plate and set one in front of Logan. "Mama hated the farm. I think she figured we were old enough to take care of ourselves."

I tried to imagine life without my meddlesome, irritating, indispensable mother. "That must have been tough."

Pete shrugged. "At first it was. But it got better."

Brynne gave her brother a tender look and handed him a plate. "What he's not telling you about is the boatload of therapy Dad made us do. Or about our mutual predilection for men who abandon us."

Pete scowled at her and sank onto the stool next to mine. "Enough about us. Are both your folks still alive?"

"My mom's relatively happy and healthy. She lives in the northern suburbs of Milwaukee, and I see her on holidays."

Brynne frowned. "What about your father?"

I shrugged. "Every now and then he sends me a pamphlet from JONAH—the Orthodox Jewish organization that claims to cure homosexuality—so I assume he's still alive."

"Ouch." Pete rested his hand on my arm.

I blinked at him. When I told Jack about my dad, he gave me a long lecture on religious tolerance that left me feeling guilty, angry, and confused about the meaning of the word *tolerant*. Pete's unqualified sympathy filled me with a rush of unexpected emotion, which I didn't want to examine or feel at the dinner table. I focused on the food, and the smell of bubbling cheese coming from the frittata on my plate made my mouth water. I took a bite. "Oh my God, this is delicious."

Pete beamed. "Logan's been experimenting with cheese making."

I stared at the kid. "You made this?"

He blushed and ducked his head. "It's not hard."

"You've worked a long time to get the cheeses just right. You should be proud of yourself." Brynne patted his arm. She turned to me. "As you can guess, we have a lot of milk. We've been selling it to a corporation, but since we can't get organic certification, the price they offer isn't enough to keep us going. If we can develop a line of simple cheeses, we could sell those at the market for more."

I looked around the table. "You're running the classic eighteenth-century farm. You don't sew your old underwear into quilts, do you?"

Pete scooped salad onto his plate and passed the bowl to me. "That's a nice image, cozying up with Brynne's lacy panties or Logan's smelly socks. It's not like we're old-fashioned. I love my diesel tractor, and we're in negotiations with the power company to install a couple of windmills behind the barn."

"They really made quilts from underwear?" Logan asked, taking the salad bowl from me.

I nodded. "Although, to be fair, what they called underwear was more like long johns than your mom's panties."

Brynne laughed. "Can we stop talking about my underwear? You guys are creeping me out. And for your information—"

Pete held up his hand. "Don't finish that sentence. Inquiring minds really do not want to know."

"Gross." Logan scowled at his mom.

The whole scene was achingly wholesome. I had a hard time believing it was real. As we ate, I tried to imagine laughing over dinner with a lover in my mother's house, not to mention introducing Pete to my dad. I couldn't picture it, but trying made my chest ache with wanting it.

* * * *

Pete's room—a small bedroom on the second floor that overlooked the barn—smelled like him, earthy and fresh. He pulled two pairs of pajama pants from the bottom drawer of an old wooden bureau and handed one to me.

"It's been a while since Logan came in unannounced, but I always wear them just in case." He bit his lip. "Um, maybe we don't need them right away. Just drop those within easy reach."

I shook them out, blue cotton with tiny white dots. I glanced toward the door. "Does it lock?"

Pete grabbed a ladder-back chair and braced it under the doorknob. "Best I can do for tonight." He stepped toward me, gliding his hand around the back of my neck and pulling me into a kiss, our tongues meeting with accustomed passion. When we broke, he cupped my jaw and smiled. "I'm really glad you're here."

I leaned my face into his hand. "Me too."

The small double bed under the window was covered with a deep red comforter. It wasn't as hot as in the city, but hot enough. We climbed out of our clothes, turned back the comforter, and lay on top of deep blue sheets. Pete flicked off the light.

As he rolled toward me, Pete's body felt familiar in the dark, and I giggled into his neck, trying to be quiet. His skin was smooth and hot as it skimmed against mine. The illicit sense of making love on a creaky old bed with his family down the hall sent my libido into overdrive. He let his head fall back as I kissed his neck. I moved down his body. He arched into me when I sucked hard on each nipple and dragged my stomach and chest across his rigid cock. By the time I opened my mouth and let his cock glide between my lips and along my tongue, his breath was coming in little gasps. His cock filled my mouth. I let it bounce against the back of my throat, trying to take all of him in.

Pete wrapped his fingers deep in my hair, his hips thrusting up to meet me. As I reached to touch myself he pulled me off, gripping my chest and sliding me all the way up his body until his lips touched my ear.

"I want to taste you too." His whispered the words. I almost couldn't hear them, but my body did. I imagined his lips curled around my cock, and blood surged into it, hardening me even more. I nodded and turned around so I could straddle his head. I leaned to swallow Pete's cock again and gasped as I felt his tongue on my balls. I pushed his cock deep into my throat to keep from moaning as he sucked first one and then the other into his mouth, his tongue sending electric currents through them, straight to my throbbing cock. And then my cock was in his mouth, and the only sound was the slurp and suck of our mouths as excitement built between us, made fast and hard by our furtiveness, the tiny danger of being heard or caught. Coming, his cock pulsed in my mouth. He tasted sweet, like fresh hay smelled. I gulped him down, feeling my orgasm rising hard in the wake of his. I held his softening cock in my mouth and buried my head between his thighs to keep from waking the household as I came.

I rolled off him, sticky with sweat, my heart pounding. When I could breathe normally again, I sat up, pulled on the blue polka-dot pajama bottoms, tossed him his red pair, and slid into his arms. I fell asleep curled into him.

Sometime in the night he pulled the covers over both of us. He was gone when I woke. I lay looking around the room. Shelves stuffed with books of all sizes lined one wall. I limped over to check out the titles, a mix of murder mysteries, science textbooks, ecological theory and literary fiction. My gaze fell on a stack of X-Men comics from the early '90s, the same series I'd collected as a kid. I realized this must have been Pete's room back then. It was an odd, intimate feeling to know I'd had sex with a man in his childhood bedroom. I wondered what it would be like to stay here for a very long time.

Movement out the window caught my eye, and I saw Pete, Logan, and the dogs emerge from the barn. I pulled on my clothes and hobbled downstairs. The smell of coffee met me halfway.

"I've got homemade granola and yogurt, or I can cook you eggs," Brynne yelled, apparently responding to my dainty progress downstairs.

"Granola's fine." I swung into the kitchen and deposited myself on the same stool I'd used the night before. "As long as you have coffee, I'm a happy man."

"Glad to hear it. Pete deserves some happiness." She poured me coffee.

I didn't have it in me to tell her there were so many reasons I was going to break his heart.

Pete and Logan exploded into the kitchen, Homer and Lady trotting behind. Pete's smile broke over me like sunshine. I was pretty sure he was on his way to breaking my heart too.

"I'm going to take Avi home after breakfast. Anything we need in town?"

Brynne deposited food on the table. She ruffled Logan's hair. He glanced at me and ducked away from her touch. I chuckled. Even the best moms could be annoying. Brynne shrugged and focused on her brother. "There's a list. But nothing that can't wait until Wednesday."

Wednesday. Just when I'd forgotten about Jack, something reminded me.

It must have shown on my face, because Pete's eyebrows furrowed. "Are you in pain? Do you want me to redo your bandage?"

"I'll do it when I get home." I sipped my coffee and stared out the kitchen window. It looked like it might rain.

* * * *

Pete pulled into the driveway of the apartment building, parking in the same place he had when he first brought me home.

He turned toward me. "Do you want me to come up?"

I shook my head. "If you do, you won't get all those chores done today."

He ran a hand along my jaw. "That might be worth it."

I kissed his palm. "Not if the animals suffer and the crops fail."

"I had a really nice weekend." His thumb caressed my lower lip.

I sucked it into my mouth. His pupils dilated. I let his thumb go and leaned in to kiss him. "Me too," I whispered into his lips before pulling away.

I slid out of the car, slung my bag over my shoulder, grabbed the crutches, and headed toward the front door. Leaving him felt like walking into a darkened room.

Chapter Ten

Unwilling to wash Pete's scent from the sheets until the last possible moment, I waited until Wednesday morning to scrub him from the apartment. It felt like a betrayal, but I wasn't sure of whom. Maybe both of them.

It was after midnight when Jack called from the road. He sounded cheerful, but when he stormed through the door two hours later, his face was rigid lines and planes. He threw his briefcase on an armchair and stomped into the kitchen.

I followed and found him peering into the refrigerator. "Are you okay?"

"You didn't used to keep this much fucking food in here. Where's the goddamned beer? Never mind, I found it." He slammed the fridge door closed with his foot as he twisted off the bottle cap. Pausing with the bottle halfway to his mouth, he added, "Did you want one?"

I shook my head. A quote from Thomas Paine floated through my mind: "The summer soldier and the sunshine patriot will, in this crisis, shrink from the service of his country; but he that stands by it now, deserves the love...."

But of course Paine was talking about the Revolutionary War, not a fuming man darkening his kitchen.

"You want to talk about it?" I asked warily. Had he somehow found out about Pete? The thought was frightening, but at the same time seemed to settle the restlessness in my gut. I was struck by the realization that the affair with Jack was over for me. I needed to start looking for another place to live. This wasn't a teeter-totter I wanted to stay on. I hoped no one would get hurt when I jumped off.

Jack drained his beer and reached into the fridge for another. He opened it, leaned against the kitchen counter, and considered me. My hair was still wet from the shower, and my sweats hung low on my hips. Jack's gaze traveled down my bare chest and settled on the pooch of my crotch. "You look hot. Like you want to get fucked. Is that what you need? My dick up your ass."

My chest relaxed. Whatever he was pissed about, it didn't have anything to do with me. His words were straight out of a porno. Jack must have been hitting some late-night Internet in Eagle River.

"Say it." His jaw tightened, and his free hand went for his belt buckle.

I could feel myself blush. I felt like an actor with a really bad script. This was a superficial, mean-guy shadow of sex with Pete. "Yeah, I want you to fuck me, to fuck my ass."

I sounded ridiculous.

He gestured toward the bedroom. "Get yourself ready. I'll be in as soon as I finish this beer."

I almost didn't do it. I felt finished with the whole thing. I couldn't quite shake the image of Jack-shaped bruises on Peggy's neck, or her certainty that I was another victim in his path. But everyone deserved a good-bye fuck. I limped past him into the bedroom and shucked my clothes.

Get yourself ready. Did that mean he wanted me lubed up before he got there? I opened the bedside table drawer and retrieved the lube, leaving it open so he could get his own condom. It was a silly line to draw in the sand, but silly lines are sometimes the only way to maintain any dignity.

I knelt on the bed, glancing down at my flaccid penis. I cast around for an image to help me out. The memory of Pete, his fingers buried deep in his own ass, did the trick. I thought I might be able to come just picturing his slick hand moving in and out. Maybe what I needed was to give Jack that same show—one last blowout image of me to take with him into the rest of his life.

I had a finger up my ass as Jack entered the bedroom. He stood still, watching me finger fuck myself. I turned away to give him a better show and to lose myself in my own thoughts.

"Oh, yeah." His voice sounded ragged, and I looked over my shoulder to see him tossing off clothes like they burned him. He opened the lower drawer and pulled out his restraints.

I stopped what I was doing. "Jack, I don't—"

He hefted his engorged penis with one hand and gestured with the restraints with the other. "If you want some of this, you'll do exactly what I tell you."

I bit my lower lip, tempted again to call it off. I looked into his eyes and saw longing and something like tenderness that jibed with the set of his jaw. I nodded, crawled onto the bed, and spread my arms so he could cuff them.

The fur was soft against my wrists. He pulled the restraints as tight as the last time, but when I protested, he backed the buckles off a notch.

"Jesus, you look hot," he whispered once he had me positioned the way he wanted, arms spread, knees bent, my head on a pillow and ass in the air. "Slutty."

He knelt behind me, his thighs pressed against mine, his cock caressing my balls. He kneaded my ass cheeks as words tumbled from him onto my back. He lobbed out a long flow of phrases, all on the same theme about what a sexy, wanton thing I was.

He leaned over me, and I could hear him rummaging in the bedside table drawer. Suddenly he froze against me. "What the fuck?"

I turned my head, straining to see him from my position. "What's wrong?"

"Condoms are missing. Four of them."

I stared at him. He counted condoms?

His glare hit me full force, and I shrank into the pillow.

He roared, "You brought someone here? You little shit." I felt his hand on my shoulder, and before I could say anything to stop him, he yanked me toward him.

I screamed at the pain. It hurt like he was ripping off my arm.

Jack dropped me immediately. "Oh, Christ. I'm sorry, I'm sorry," he kept murmuring as he fumbled with the cuff at my wrist. Every movement jostled my arm, sending bolts of pain through my shoulder.

Once Jack had unhooked me, I lay for a few minutes trying to breathe, my ass still in the air and my arm a dead fish on the mattress next to me. Stabilizing my shoulder from underneath with my good arm, I inched back until I was sitting on my heels, only vaguely aware of the pain it caused my ankle. Jack was pacing beside the bed, *shit* and *sorry* and *fuck* dribbling out of his mouth in a steady stream. I held on to my arm and searched for a shoulder position I could tolerate. Waves of nausea pulsed through me whenever I moved.

My teeth chattered, and I started to shake.

"Jack." My voice was barely above a whisper, and I had to say it three times before he stopped pacing and looked at me. "Help me get up."

He sprinted toward the bed and grasped my good arm. I hissed with pain, and he slowed, his touch gentler. With him under my good shoulder and his arm around my waist, I was able to move off my heels, propel myself forward, and eventually sit on the edge of the bed. Jack draped a blanket over my shoulders. It felt like I'd run a marathon.

He resumed his pacing. He'd moved from cursing to whole phrases, like *this can't happen* and *fucking impossible*. I pulled the blanket closed and tuned him out, concentrating on stopping my shaking and figuring out how to breathe without passing out from the pain every time I inhaled.

"Jack." This time I got his attention. "I need to go to the emergency room."

"No." He stood over me, hands on his hips.

I looked up at him, startled, and the movement produced another wave of nausea. I concentrated on my breath, inhaling and exhaling, my gaze on his belly button and limp cock. When I was certain I wouldn't puke, I asked, "What do you mean, no? I need to go to the hospital."

He knelt in front of me, still shaking his head. "I'm sorry, Avi, but we can't do that. Reporters hang around emergency rooms waiting for a story. It would ruin me."

I gritted my teeth. "So call me a cab. I'm fucking hurt, Jack. You need to take care of me."

He patted my thigh, his voice soft. "I will, Avi. I promise. But emergency rooms mean questions, reporters, even police. How would you explain this? We'll get you help. But not at an emergency room. A private doctor. Someone discreet."

I glanced at the watch on his wrist, which rested on my knee. "It's four in the morning. Nothing else is open. You're suggesting I wait until morning like this?"

He gazed up at me, and I realized it was the first time I'd ever seen him on his knees. His voice dripped honey. "I'll get you some ibuprofen. You want tea, or how about I make you a nice cup of hot chocolate? You'll be feeling better in no time."

I stared at him. Hot chocolate? What did he think I was, ten? I glanced down at my taped ankle. It was like my left side was crumpling at the joints, first my ankle, now my shoulder. Immobilizing. His jaw was set. My options appeared to be very limited. I was trapped. I doubted I'd be able to dress without his help. And I sure as hell couldn't afford an emergency room visit on my own. A private doctor. I remembered Dr. Stella Goldstein's pleasant face and hoped her office opened early.

I sighed. "Open that bottle of single malt scotch the governor gave you for Christmas. If I'm stuck here, the least you can do is give me a drink."

"Peggy wanted to save that."

I gritted my teeth. "Buy her another. It's not engraved, is it?"

He paled, and for a moment, I thought he'd refuse. But he must have realized his options were limited too, because he nodded and trotted toward the kitchen, reappearing in a minute with scotch, two glasses, and a bottle of ibuprofen. I made him shake four pills into my good hand, and I swallowed them down with half a tumbler of excellent scotch. I held out my glass for a refill. Jack poured us each a healthy slug and slumped against the wall to watch me.

"I really am sorry, Avi. I never meant to hurt you."

"Well, you did." I sipped the scotch. It tasted smoky and smooth, but the pain lapped up the alcohol. No way I'd be able to get drunk.

Jack slid down the wall and sat, arms resting on his knees. We both watched the light bounce through amber liquid as he swirled his glass.

His gaze met mine, his brown eyes darker than usual. "On my way down here, I got an anonymous text demanding control over my vote on the organic certification law. If I don't vote the way they want, they'll expose me. Whoever they are, they claim to have witnesses and proof."

"About us?" I stared at him incredulously. "About me?"

He shrugged. "It doesn't matter. I'll have to give in. What else can I do?"

Who knew about us? Isaac? But what would Isaac care about farming law? I closed my eyes as the world shifted and pieces fell into place. Organic certification. Blackmail.

Pete's voice echoed in my head. *"Is the assemblyman coming down tonight?"*

No way would Pete betray me like that. No matter how important the organic certification was. I could hear Pete—*if the damned certification law doesn't get repealed...."* Pete was too good to be true. And, like my mother always said, if it's too good to be true, it's not.

I downed my scotch and held out my glass for more. Maybe if I drank enough, I could pass out and be done with this damned night. I drained that glass in one shot. The scotch warmed my chest on the way down and left me dizzy.

My mind filled with images of Pete—Pete looking at Jack's picture, Pete looking at the bruises on my wrists, Pete fingering the family photo. Pete asking me to lobby Jack.

When had Pete decided he wanted more than a hook-up with me, before or after he learned about Jack? My stomach twisted. At least Jack had only used me for sex.

"I think I should lie down." Moving sounded like the worst possible idea, but I didn't think I'd be able to stay sitting up. "I'll need your help."

Jack jumped up, his face pale.

"Careful," I spat as he bumped me. I bit down hard on the hurt and let him help me turn on to my back. My shoulder hit the bed with a spike of pain, which gradually fell into a throb. I looked at Jack. We were both still naked, and I suddenly didn't want to be that vulnerable around him. "Get my sweatpants. I'm fucking freezing here."

Phrases I'd heard out at the farm tumbled into my consciousness.

"We're in a Catch-22."

"A bill or two away from having to let the place go."

"Can't afford, can't afford, can't afford."

Who knew better than I did how money, or the lack of it, corrupts? I thought of Logan and Brynne and the well-kept farm always on the brink of financial disaster because they couldn't get certification. How far would Pete go to protect his family and the farm?

What had he told Isaac at breakfast? *"I'd do just about anything to keep from having to sell."* Understanding splashed through me like cold water. He'd only been hanging out with me to blackmail Jack. Compared to taking care of his family and the farm, I was nothing, a means to an end. It looked like everything between us had been a fake and Pete was as much of a whore as I was, only this time I was the fool who paid. I wanted to puke.

* * * *

I could hear Jack moving around the apartment, the whisper of a drawer opening, the clack of hangers against the metal closet bar. Water ran in the bathroom, the shower. The minty smell of his shampoo tickled my nose. Traffic noises increased outside. A garbage truck clattered to a stop by the building. Such a regular sound. It had to be seven o'clock Thursday morning.

I opened my eyes. Jack was staring down at me, dressed in a blue suit and holding out a cup of coffee. "We should get you ready to go."

I sat up, engaging my abs in a slow sit-up, swung my legs over the side of the bed, and took the coffee from Jack.

Coffee with cream. Two years together and he'd never noticed I drank my coffee black. I sighed and sipped. Didn't matter. It was warm and wet. I closed my eyes and drank down the cup.

Jack took my empty cup and stood, fidgeting. "I've been looking in the phone book for a doctor near here. There's one a few blocks away."

I started to shake my head, thought better of it, and said, "I've got a doctor. Her card's in my wallet on the bureau. I can't afford the deductible. You'll have to cover that."

He nodded vigorously. "Yes, of course, of course." He strode to the bureau and began riffling through my wallet. Pete's card was in there, and I wondered if he'd notice it crammed in among the dozen or so other cards. Pete, his betrayer and mine. At least the damage Jack inflicted was only physical.

I used one crutch to hoist myself up. My shoulder screamed at the loss of my right arm as a brace. "I need something as a sling."

He startled me by ripping a long strip of fabric from the top sheet. Something else he'd be replacing before Peggy came down again. Between us, we used it to anchor my arm. Jack glanced at his watch and cleared his throat. "I'm sorry about this. I'll take you, and of course I'll pay, but I can't wait. The risk is too great."

I stared at him. He had the grace to look away.

"I don't think I can get a shirt over this." I kept my voice level, polite like my mother taught me. "There's a zippered hoodie in the bottom drawer. Would you get that, please?" While Jack rummaged for my sweatshirt, I looked at my sneakers. Obviously I was on my own from here on out. I limped toward the closet and toed into my flip-flops. Jack draped the jacket over my shoulders, helped me slip my good arm through the sleeve, and zipped it up with my wounded arm on the inside.

I slid my wallet, keys, and phone into the pocket and pulled the hood up over my unkempt hair. If I was going to look like a thug, at least I could do it with relative anonymity.

Jack fiddled with his jacket, and I realized he didn't want to be seen with me leaving the building. I closed my eyes in self-condemnation as I rescued him one last time. "Why don't you go down and bring the car around? I'll meet you at the curb."

I felt once again like a wounded soldier as I thudded my slow progress from apartment to street. Each step sent a jolt of pain through my shoulder and a duller throb to my ankle. The situation took "sorry for myself" to a whole new dimension.

The car idled at the curb as I hit the automatic door-opening button with my crutch. He didn't get out but pushed open the passenger door as I neared. I handed him the crutch and lowered myself onto the seat as carefully as I could. I slammed the door closed with a wince.

Jack pulled away and started down the hill. I could feel every bump in my shoulder and squinted against the pain. We didn't speak. The car slowed. I opened my eyes long enough to see that we were passing through the ATM line at a bank. Jack's face was grim as he punched in the numbers, no doubt working out what lie he'd offer Peggy about his extra expenses. The machine dispensed bills with a whir.

Trading sex for cash hadn't been among my career goals. But the Torah is full of stories of compromised virtue. Lot offered his virgin daughters up to the crowd to rape. Ruth seduced her employer. Even Noah, the only righteous man of his time, ended up drunk in bed with his son. It's there in every religious tradition. The Christians have Mary Magdalene, and the Buddha was a player in his youth.

I put out my hand, and he handed it all over.

"I can give you more later. The machine won't let me take out more than five hundred dollars a day."

I looked at the wad of bills and then at him. "Thank you."

He nodded and kept his eyes on the road.

I stuffed the money into my pocket and watched out the window as we circled Lake Monona. Wind kicked up whitecaps on the lake. Three old black men fished off a pier in the bay. Just like a normal day except for the way I hurt all over—inside and out.

Stella Goldstein's building was a low stucco structure set back from the street. Jack pulled to the curb. He glanced at his watch. "They should open soon. We can drive around the block until then."

"No." The last thing I wanted was more time with Jack. I opened the car door. "I'll be back to get my stuff as soon as I can. I'll leave my key on the table."

His eyes scanned my face.

I maneuvered the crutch out of the car. "Don't worry. I'm not your Monica Lewinsky." Before he could say anything, I hoisted myself out onto the sidewalk. Gritting my teeth against the pain, I limped toward the front office door. I listened to the engine idling at the curb for a long moment. The gears engaged, and he drove off.

In the glass door, I could see myself lumbering forward like some pathetic victim. I peered inside and found a clock on the far wall. Quarter to eight. I looked around. No benches for waiting outside. I leaned against the glass, balanced with the crutch, and let myself slide to the ground. I had a few minutes with nothing to do but contemplate the mess I'd made of my life.

Almost immediately, a white sedan pulled into the lot next to the clinic. I watched Doc Stella hurry from the parking lot, her eyes down as she dug in her purse. She'd tied her long black hair into a ponytail and wore pressed black slacks rather than jeans, but it was her. She looked up, spotted me, and froze. I didn't blame her. I must have looked like a street person, sprawled on the cement by her door, a hoodie covering my face.

"Hi," I called, brushing back the hood so she could see me. "Avi Rosen, sprained ankle at the farmers' market."

"You're Pete's friend?" She hurried forward. "What happened?"

"It's my shoulder. I think it's dislocated."

She squatted, her gaze assessing. "Should I call the police?"

"No. But you could help me stand up, if you wanted to."

She nodded. Wrapping my good arm over her shoulder and her arm under my waist, she helped me rise first to my knees and then to my feet.

She unlocked the door. "How did you get here?"

"A friend dropped me off."

She shook her head. "Some friend."

"Yeah."

She took me straight through the waiting room, tastefully decorated in shades of blue and white, and into the standard patient room. After having me swallow a few painkillers, she helped me up onto the exam table and disappeared, returning with a dark blue cotton blanket, which she draped over me. "I have a few tasks that need doing before the day starts. As soon as my nurse gets here, we'll look at that shoulder. In the meantime, try to relax."

I lay staring at the ceiling, waiting for the drugs to kick in. Eventually a nurse came in, helped me out of my sweatshirt, and re-covered me with the blanket. Closing my eyes, I tried to imagine my life when the messy present was done. Maybe I'd get a job out west, where there were mountains and streams and everyone lived in peace. I drifted off picturing myself lecturing in a smoking jacket, pipe in hand while classical music played softly in the background and hot young men looked at me adoringly, taking furious notes.

Voices in the hallway woke me. Moments later I opened my eyes to find Doc Stella leaning over me.

She peeled off the blanket. "You think it's dislocated. Has this happened before?"

I grunted, "No." And I planned to spend the rest of my life making sure nothing like this hellish night happened again.

Doc Stella peered at my shoulder. "That's some bruise you've got going. You want to tell me what happened?"

No. I did not.

At my silence, she glanced at my face. "I'm not easily shocked, Avi. The bruising tells me this happened sometime in the middle of the night. You're not intoxicated, so I'm guessing you didn't jump from the second-story window in a frat house."

I raised an eyebrow.

She nodded. "Right, I didn't take you for a frat boy. Given the timing, my second guess is that this is the result of a sexual adventure gone wrong. Am I getting warm?" She touched my wrist. "Nasty bruise here too. Bondage?"

I nodded, shame welling in my chest.

Her voice softened. "It's all right. I'm here to heal, not to judge. Tell me what happened so I can help."

I stumbled through an explanation of the night's events, leaving out the particulars of who and why. While I talked, Doc Stella poked and prodded, the physical pain almost a relief.

When I finished, she patted my thigh. "I think you're right. It's a dislocation. I'll need to see an X-ray before I do anything else, but in the meantime, I'll send my nurse in with something more for the pain." She paused, her gaze on mine. "It's none of my business, of course, but whoever he is, he should be here holding your hand."

I blinked hard. The last thing I wanted to do was compound my humiliation by crying. "He had to work," I croaked.

"Do I need to stop buying my vegetables from Jakobsen's?"

"No. It's not Pete." His was a deeper betrayal.

"Good." She gave a quick nod. "I'd hate to give up those strawberries, and I like to support local agriculture. I know the Jakobsens are always on the edge financially. It's a wonder they've kept it together for so long. But then you've probably heard even more about the whole organic certification mess than I have." She looked down at my leg. "As long as you're here, I'll get an X-ray of that ankle too." And with that she was gone.

The nurse arrived with a syringe, and moments later I was floating on a numbed cloud, wondering how I could have been so stupid. Even Pete's customers knew how important organic certification was to the survival of Jakobsen's Farms.

The X-rays went by in a blur, and I drifted in pain-free misery until Doc Stella appeared again, rolling a computer over by my exam table.

She pointed toward the skeletal image of a foot that filled the computer screen. "The good news is that your ankle looks like it's healing well. I don't see any complications. I'll have the nurse re-tape it before you go, and keep doing whatever you're doing."

"Spelling out historical documents," I muttered, fascinated by the sight of my bones in black and white.

Doc Stella raised her eyebrows. "Civics lessons as rehabilitation. Interesting. Here's the bad news." She hit a button, and a different set of bones appeared. The head of my arm bone looked unconnected to anything else. The image made me a little nauseated.

"It's dislocated?"

She nodded. "And I'm afraid we're going to have to put it back." She looked at the nurse, who stuck another needle in my arm. After a minute, Doc Stella touched me. I couldn't feel anything. "Okay?"

I watched in sick fascination as she rotated the bone. I could see the head moving around under my skin like something out of *Alien*. With a loud *pop*, it slammed into place. Doc Stella did some more joint wiggling and stepped back. "That should do it. Keep it immobile for two weeks, after which I want to see you back here. We'll get you fitted with a proper sling, and I'll write a prescription for pain meds. When the morphine wears off, that's going to hurt like crazy. Do you have someone to call who can take you home?"

Home. I blinked at her. The thought of going back to the apartment, of seeing Jack, turned my stomach. "Yeah, I do."

"Good." She paused at the door and looked back at me. "And try to be careful. You're running out of body parts."

I thumbed my phone. Isaac answered on the third ring and agreed to pick me up.

The nurse fitted me with an elaborate sling, wrapped my ankle in a fresh bandage, and helped me into my hoodie. I told her to trash the ragged strip of sheet.

I walked outside, and I called Pete. He answered, his voice full of sunshine and fields of clover.

For a moment, I wondered if I was wrong, if Pete really wasn't blackmailing Jack. So I asked him, "Just how important is the organic certification thing to you?"

He sighed, and all the light went out of his voice. "I don't know if we'll make it without certification. That's why I've been lobbying your assemblyman. His vote is extremely important."

Lobbying? That was a new name for it. "That's no excuse," I mumbled into the phone. "You had no right."

"What are you talking about?" Did he sound defensive or confused? I couldn't tell. I'd been a fucking fool to trust someone I didn't know the first thing about.

I was totally disgusted with us both. "You know damned well what I'm talking about. You used me."

Pete's voice rose. "Avi, where are you? What's going on?"

"Fuck you, Mr. Innocent." I clicked shut the phone before the tears that were threatening to come could overwhelm me.

The phone buzzed. Pete's number lit up the screen. I pushed *End*, stuffed the thing in my pocket, and hobbled to the street to wait for Isaac.

I found a tree to lean against. Traffic trickled by. Clouds blocked the sun. I felt tired and angry and very alone.

Chapter Eleven

Isaac pulled into the apartment building parking lot. "This is crazy. You should be in bed."

The faint rumblings of distant pain in my shoulder told me he was probably right. Still. "It won't take long, and I need to get my crap out of there."

He looked at me, his dark eyes serious. "Okay. Let's do it."

When I'd taken Jack up on his offer of a place to stay, I hauled most of my belongings over to Milwaukee for storage in my mother's basement. I lived lightly in Jack's apartment. My entire wardrobe fit in a couple of suitcases, and aside from what was in the backpack and messenger bag, I kept a box of papers for The Project in the back bedroom.

I was useless and spacey. While I poured out the story, Isaac packed my clothes and, at my direction, emptied what was left of Pete's food into a grocery bag and filled another with my frozen potpies and ramen noodles. At the last minute, I grabbed the pillow from my side of the bed. I knew from experience how lumpy the couch in Isaac's basement was. I left the condoms and lube. Jack could clean up for himself the next time Peggy came to town.

Isaac crammed my stuff into the backseat of his battered sedan. I looked at my mangled bike, still locked to the bike rack beside the apartment building.

Isaac's gaze followed mine. "Too bad we don't know anyone with a truck."

"I'm not calling him."

He looked at me skeptically. "You don't know that he's Jack's anonymous texter. That's the point of anonymity."

"Oh, come on, it's obvious."

Isaac opened the driver's door. "I still think you should call him."

"Fuck him." Sliding into the passenger seat, I silently promised my bike I'd come back for it later. It wasn't like I'd be riding soon anyway.

Isaac's house was uncharacteristically quiet when we arrived. Which was good because all I wanted to do was crawl into that mildewed cave of a basement and lick my wounds. We left the food in the kitchen as a house present, and I limped down the stairs, my shoulder starting to throb. I dropped onto the couch, and Isaac piled my crap nearby. He looked at his watch. "I have to get to class, but I'll come back right after. Anything I can bring?"

I shook my head. "You're great, you know that?"

He nodded. "That's what they say."

He bounded up the stairs, and I was alone in semidarkness, the only light two tiny windows high in the far wall. The basement smelled of mold and beer. My shoulder was starting to seriously ache. I dry swallowed one of the heavy-duty painkillers Doc Stella had prescribed. I should have made Isaac bring me down some water. It was humiliating to be this helpless. This fucking helpless.

I pulled the remainder of the money Jack had thrust at me out of my pocket and counted. After my fifty-dollar co-pay at the pharmacy, I was down to four-fifty. Of course, I owed Doc Stella two hundred of that, but that bill would need to make the insurance circuit and wouldn't be due for another few months. The last time I'd checked my bank account there'd been maybe one-fifty in it. It was the end of June. I had six weeks to finish the draft of my dissertation so I could earn some money in the fall. My other choices were to throw myself on the mercy of my mother and move back home, or get a job that involved asking, "Do you want fries with that?" I was almost thirty years old and had two dozen years of education, but unless I finished The Project, I wasn't qualified for anything else.

I stuffed my money back in my pocket and lay on the lumpy, beer- and semen-encrusted couch feeling sorry for myself until the painkiller kicked in and I drifted into fitful sleep.

* * * *

"Food and drink. Sorry, no alcohol with your pain pills," Isaac announced as he came down the stairs later that night. He was carrying a sandwich, a beer and a can of soda. My stomach grumbled, reminding me it had been almost twenty-four hours since my last meal.

Of course, I'd been sleeping on and off for most of that time. The couch was bumpy and smelled like mildew and sweat, but with my arm propped on my wadded-up sweatshirt and my foot on the armrest, it had been good enough. I'd been up a few times to pee in the disgusting toilet in one corner of the laundry room, but other than that, I'd stayed on the couch in my drug-induced fog.

"Hey." I struggled to sit, the ache in my arm reasserting itself with the move.

"How you doing?" He settled on the floor in front of me.

"You mean other than being jobless, homeless, loveless, broke, and crippled?" I took the sandwich from him.

He popped open the soda and set it by my good ankle. He opened his beer and took a long pull. "Yeah, I can see how that would be a downer. If it helps, we had an impromptu house meeting, and the guys agreed to rent you this space for fifty bucks a month. Renting out the basement is a complete violation of the lease, so it's not official, but if you donate the money to the beer fund jar every month, no one will be the wiser." He looked down at his feet. "Um, and if you don't have the cash, we can loan it."

I nudged his toe with my good foot. "I'm not that broke."

"Good." He sounded relieved. "And who knows? Maybe you'll like it. Ted moves out at the end of August, and you could take his place."

I took a bite of the sandwich—tomato and cheese on what must have been the last of the bread Pete left. It tasted so good I thought I might cry.

Isaac watched me devour the sandwich. "On your list of woes, I'm not sure about loveless. I mean, I know you and Jack are over, but what about—"

I stopped him. "I don't want to talk about it. I know the whole thing about repealing the organic certification law is important to him, but what about loyalty? Trust?"

"You don't know—"

"Stop. What I need to do is move on." I decided not to lick the plate and washed down the sandwich with a long swallow of sicky sweetness. "Finish The Project on time, get my degree and find a job at some fine university far, far away."

Isaac shrugged. He lifted his beer and toasted, "To The Project."

I clinked his bottle with my soda can. "May she find her completion and let me go."

* * * *

It took me a few days to function without painkillers, and three more to master the art of one-handed typing. Isaac helped me rig a desk from a board and two sawhorses someone had abandoned in the basement. He hauled down a kitchen chair, and I was in business, pounding through the accumulation of years of research. My days took on a rhythm—coffee at the sunny kitchen table with Isaac, Nathan and whoever else was around, after which I'd hobble down to my crypt and work until feet pounding above me let me know dinner was happening. After that more work, until I couldn't keep my eyes open and I lumbered to my couch to sleep. I completed spelling exercises with my foot, tossed money in the food and beer kitties, and wiped the counters and table after dinner, the only household task that could be efficiently done with one hand.

Pete quit calling. Jack seemed to have vanished. I tried hard not to think of either of them and to lose myself in a world of powdered wigs and gunpowder, where political corruption was reduced to dusty old stories. Chapters took shape, arguments formed, and the word count grew. As much as possible, I disappeared into the story of a band of agnostics and clergy, merchants and farmers, abolitionists and slaveholders, who, having formed their more perfect union, engaged in a messy, sometimes brave, sometimes traitorous battle over how to make a nation.

Like a burrowing animal, I lived in dark and cool while the outside world sweated through summer.

* * * *

Sun streamed in through the kitchen windows. Those with regular jobs, like Nathan, had left. The two men who worked the night shift had stumbled through on their way to bed, and everyone else was still sleeping. I brought the pot to the table and poured Isaac and myself more coffee. My shoulder still hurt, but at least I was walking without crutches.

Isaac thumped the paper. "Your assemblyman made a big speech yesterday."

"Not my assemblyman." I slid into the chair opposite him.

He sipped his coffee, frowned, and added three teaspoons of sugar. "Whatever. He came out in support of the organic certification law."

I closed my eyes. The mention of that stupid legislation made me want to jump back into the eighteenth century. "You mean, he came out in favor of repealing the law."

Isaac folded the paper open with a crack and shoved it at me. "No. That's not what I meant. Read the friggin' article."

I took it from him and stared uncomprehendingly at the heading. ORGANIC CERTIFICATION: JACK KRAUSMAN SUPPORTS THE STATUS QUO. I scanned the article, the rest of the paper, looking for the damage control piece that had to be there, the one that would cover Jack's ass when Pete outed him. It wasn't there. "I don't get it."

Isaac looked at me over his coffee cup. "Did Jack say which side the threat came from?"

I closed my eyes, scanned my memory, trying to dredge up our exact conversation. *"Whoever they are, they claim to have witnesses and proof."*

"About us? About me?"

Jack had said, *"It doesn't matter. I'll have to give in. What else can I do?"*

I opened my eyes and looked at Isaac. "But who else would know?"

He shrugged. "Maybe you weren't the only boy in his stable."

I blinked.

I thumbed my phone. Jack answered on the second ring.

"Am I going to read my name in the papers soon, Jack?"

"Wait a minute." Muffled sounds followed, ending in the distinct clack of a door closing. Jack's voice rasped in my ear. "Avi? What are you talking about? Are you threatening me?"

"Am I threatening you? No, of course not. I read about your speech in this morning's papers and—"

"I can't talk here. Meet me in"—I could almost hear him check his watch—"an hour. Somewhere inconspicuous, like the arboretum."

"You're kidding." Isaac looked at me, and I rolled my eyes. "Jack, my arm's still in a sling, and my ankle aches after walking a block. I'm not traipsing through the arboretum like we're in some John le Carré novel."

He cleared his throat. "Right, um, where are you? I'll come there."

I gave him the address.

* * * *

Jack and his suit looked supremely out of place in the shabby living room. He perched uncomfortably on the threadbare couch, his hands grasping his kneecaps like he was trying to keep them in place.

I settled into a straight-back chair across from him. What had I ever seen in him?

His gaze skittered across my sling. "How have you been?"

"I've been better. But I'm healing."

He nodded. "Are you going to the newspapers?"

I shook my head. "No. But aren't you about to get outed because of your stand on organic certification?"

He jerked back. "Christ, no. That's the point. I made that speech. I'll vote the way they tell me to. What else can they want?"

I stared at him, my mouth dry. "Let me get this straight. The blackmail was to keep you from voting to rescind the law?"

He nodded.

So Isaac was right. It wasn't Pete. I sat up straight for the first time in a long time. "You weren't being blackmailed by the organic farmers?"

At the look of confusion on his face, I was engulfed by a wave of guilt as big as the Mississippi flood of 1927. I pictured Pete's face, open, smiling and, yes, honest. What had made me think he could be anything other than the great guy he was? Clearly I'd been focusing on history's underbelly for too long.

He frowned. "Why would you think that?"

I let that go. "How did they know about you?"

He had the decency to blush. "I, uh, visited a private club a few times. There are pictures." He rubbed his hands along his thighs and peered at me. "How much money do you need to stay away from the papers?"

I grimaced. "I told you, I'm not threatening you. I owe that much to Peggy and the boys."

"Let me give you money anyway."

I thought about it. A little money might go a long way in my current circumstances. Except that I felt bad enough about myself already, and I was through being anyone's whore. "No, Jack. I don't need anything more from you. I think you should go."

He stood and, with a last searching look, walked out the door.

I held my phone for a long time, staring at Pete's number. It's a hard switch to go from betrayed to betrayer. I had a week to finish that damned draft of The Project. Maybe then I'd be ready to ask his forgiveness. I stuck the phone in my pocket and crawled back to my basement and the long ago.

* * * *

August 13—two days before Prof Joan's deadline—I glanced through the document one more time. At more than three hundred fifty pages, it felt like an unwieldy elephant trampling through my computer. The title took up half a page, and the footnotes seemed to extend into infinity. I typed her a short e-mail, attached the file, whispered something like a prayer, and hit *Send*. For better or worse, the electrons that gave shape to my dissertation were winging their way across the ether to her computer. My fate was sealed.

I stood, arching to relieve the kink in my back brought on by weeks of nights spent sleeping on the lumpy sofa and days hunched over my laptop. I rolled my shoulder carefully. It still got stiff easily, but Doc Stella assured me that would pass with a few more weeks of physical therapy. Or prescribed torture, as I preferred to call it. The house was quiet. I checked my watch—eleven in the morning. With a jolt, I realized it was Wednesday. The market would be open.

I grabbed my toilet bag, towel, and a change of clothes and started toward the stairs. I glanced at the crutches leaning against the wall. They belonged in the loft of an old red barn, and I should have returned them weeks before. The wood felt cool in my hand as I carried them up the stairway.

Climbing out of the basement was like moving from the cooler to the oven. My digs might be the most squalid in the house, but everyone else had drowned in their own sweat all summer. Maybe I wouldn't move into a real bedroom, even when one opened up. Except winter would be fucking cold underground. And I had to climb two flights to get to the shower.

I scrubbed myself clean, shaved, clipped all twenty of my nails, and wiped down the mirror so I could see myself. And I was sorry I did. After a summer in the basement, my skin looked freakishly pale, especially compared with the golden brown tan I imagined Pete would be sporting. My left arm still looked scrawny, and the whole shoulder girdle sloped down on that side. And my hair? I looked like I'd been living in a cave for a month. Probably because I had.

Turning away from the mirror, I shrugged into my T-shirt, pulled on my only clean shorts, and headed down the stairs, stopping to toss my gear into the basement on my way. I found my Top-Siders in the pile of shoes by the door and stepped out into the street, crutches slung over my shoulder like a hobo pack. My twisted wreck of a bike was tucked in a far corner of my basement hideaway, waiting for me to earn my first paycheck as either a teaching assistant or at whatever fast-food restaurant would take me if the dissertation draft didn't satisfy Prof Joan. Even bus fare was a financial stretch at the moment. But the walk would only be a couple of miles, and it felt good to be out in the sun.

The heady scent of lavender wafted toward me from a nearby garden, and a cat basked on the lawn across the street. A flock of white butterflies burst into flight as I approached a row of ornamental cabbage. I had only seventy-five dollars and change to my name. But after all these years, my dissertation was finally in Prof Joan's in-box, my thirtieth birthday was still months away, and maybe I could patch things up with Pete. Hope—an audacious thing, indeed.

As I approached University Avenue, bus fumes thickened the air. I could feel my skin reddening from the sun. My left heel rubbed against the canvas rim of the shoe. McDonald's had a sign in the window. I stopped and picked up an application, just in case.

State Street was its usual carnival, filled with old and young hippies, tourists, and shopping bag-carting young women. I climbed the hill slowly, feeling hot and sticky. A glance at my forearm told me I'd also be feeling the sunburn soon enough.

The Capitol building gleamed white. A band of gardeners was changing the flowers in the corner flower beds. Two dark-suited men deep in conversation trotted down the steps, dodging a family of tourists. I glanced at the second-floor windows, wondering if Jack was in town, and looked away. Probably not, and it didn't matter anyway.

Beyond the Capitol building, I could see the colorful market booths. Most of the vegetables would be gone by now. The vendors would be packing up soon. My heart pounded in my temples. My breathlessness had nothing to do with the walk.

I spotted Pete almost immediately, tall and muscular, laughing with a customer. He saw me, and the laugh died. His eyes took on a wariness I hadn't seen before. The woman holding a bunch of carrots turned, following his gaze. She looked at me and back at him, dropped a wad of money on the table, and moved on.

"Hey." I held out the crutches. "I brought these back." Well, that was obvious enough. Maybe next I'd tell him how hot it was. Or how hot he was.

He looked at the crutches like he'd never seen them before. His gaze traveled to my foot. "You're all healed up? How's the shoulder?"

"My shoulder. How'd you hear about that?"

His mouth drew a straight line. "Stella asked how you were. Something in her tone worried me."

I closed my eyes. "Pete, I—"

"I called, but evidently you weren't returning my phone calls. Fortunately I had Isaac's number. He told me that asshole dislocated your shoulder. He also let me know why you were avoiding me. Your trust in me was hardly heartening. I thought we had something…. It doesn't matter." Pete fussed with a pile of radishes. A woman approached, looked at his face and mine, and veered away.

"I'm sorry."

His eyes flashed. "Sorry? Huh. Well, that fixes everything. Thanks for bringing back the crutches."

"I turned in my dissertation today."

His face softened. "Congratulations. That must feel good. And it means you're officially on the job market. Soon you'll be off to Timbuktu."

"What are you doing here?" Brynne's voice cut through the crowd.

Pete glanced at her. "Avi was just returning the crutches."

She faced me, hands on her hips. "Do you have any idea how—"

"Brynne, don't." His voice was quiet, but it stopped her. "No need to get into it now." He started loading the radishes into a box. "We better get going. Plenty to do back at the farm."

I started to speak. It physically hurt to stand there watching him box vegetables with so much unsaid between us. I turned and walked away. The trip back home felt like trudging through mud.

Chapter Twelve

Prof Joan's door was closed. I stood in the dark, wood-paneled hallway with my heart pounding. I checked my watch and raised my fist to knock.

"Come."

I pushed open the door. She looked up and seemed pleased to see me. A wave of relief broke over me, so intense that I thought my knees might give out. She gestured to a chair, and I fell into it gratefully.

She retrieved a stack of papers and plunked it down on her desk. My incredibly long and pretentious title spilled across the top page. "I'm old-fashioned enough that I print everything out."

I could feel myself flushing. "I'm sorry. I think I knew that. I should have brought you a hard copy."

"No problem. The department can afford to print the odd dissertation or two." Her eyes narrowed as she scanned me. "You've lost weight, and you're pale. Are you well?"

I shrugged. "I'm okay." I nodded toward the pile on her desk. "What did you think?"

She beamed. Beamed. "I knew you could do it. Cogent, articulate and well reasoned. I've some notes, of course, but I see no reason you can't defend this semester." She started flipping through her date book. "Shall we schedule it for the last week in October?"

I stared at her. "Really?"

"Yes, really. And we should talk about what you'll do after. I have something that might interest you." She rummaged in her desk drawer and brought out a single sheet of paper. She slid it across the desk to me.

"The community college?" I could hear the hurt in my voice. Prof Joan's students went on to teach at prestigious institutions, to lecture to the future leaders of the nation or to have brilliant careers in public service. Teaching at the two-year institution down the road didn't qualify as academic glory.

She sat back in her chair, tapping her tented fingers against her lips. Her voice was full of compassion when she spoke. "It's a good job, Avi." She nodded toward my dissertation, which seemed to wilt on her desk. "Your work is excellent. You could turn this into a book, perhaps even a popular one. But I didn't get the sense you enjoyed writing it. Did you?"

I glanced at the pile of papers and shook my head. "No, not really."

"You're excellent in the classroom. Students love you. You like teaching. Am I right?"

I nodded.

She contemplated me. "Don't let your ego get in the way of your happiness. Keep doing research for your own enjoyment, even publishing if you like. But I think you'll be happiest in a job where you can focus on teaching. Assuming the defense goes well, which I'm sure it will, you'll graduate in December. They're looking for someone to start in January. If you don't like it, you can always put yourself back on the job market with more experience on your résumé."

As I looked at the paper in my hand, an idea started to bloom in my mind. Maybe it wouldn't be bad to stay in the Madison area. The college was close to the farmers' market.

As if reading my thoughts, Prof Joan added, "How's that nice young man I met last summer?"

I looked down. No way was I having this conversation. Shrugging, I told her, "Fine."

If she noticed my reticence, she didn't mention it. Instead she said, "In academia we don't often get to take jobs near our families."

I nodded. Benjamin Franklin once said that "energy and persistence conquer all things." And Thomas Jefferson wrote, "It takes time to persuade men to do even what is for their own good." I wondered what organic farmers did in the winter.

Prof Joan handed me yet another piece of paper. "Here's your teaching assistantship schedule for the fall. You'll be lecturing on the Civil War. It will be great practice for your new job."

* * * *

I scrambled to plan a few lectures ahead before the High Holidays. Mom wanted me home for Rosh Hashanah, which fell on a Tuesday, and that meant I'd need to have Wednesday's lecture ready before I caught the bus over. Even on Saturday morning, I should have been slaving away at my desk in a dark corner of the office I shared with three other graduate teaching assistants, instead of peddling up State Street on my newly repaired bicycle. On the other hand, the least I could do was bring Mom some apples and honey for a sweet new year. The fact that she'd probably have her own apples sliced and honey set out on the table by the time I got there wasn't important. It was the thought that counted, right? I'd spent too much of my life drifting—accepting whatever came my way. It was time to take charge of my life. Or at least to give it my best shot.

I stopped behind Pete's booth and leaned my bike against the tree. He looked as handsome as ever—his hair a blond halo, and his eyes, when he looked at me, were a darker blue, set off by his dark sweater and the wrinkles of pain around their edges. I would have given anything not to be the one who put those there.

I stepped closer, my fingers brushing the rough lip of the wooden table. "Hi."

"Hi." He stood completely still, as if afraid I might hit him.

The apples gleamed in stacks of varying shades of red. I held one to my nose and inhaled the crisp fall scent. "I want to take some apples to my mother for Rosh Hashanah. Something not too sweet."

He reached for a deep red apple. His paring knife bit into the flesh. Juice dripped down his fingers as he handed me a slice. "Liberty is nice. And the name has a Constitutional Congress ring to it."

I started, amazed he remembered. I bit into the apple, and the flesh crunched between my teeth with an explosion of sugary tartness. "I'd like honey too."

"For a sweet new year." He set a jar in front of me. "I've been hearing it all day."

I fingered the honey jar, not looking into his eyes. "Rosh Hashanah, the Jewish new year, is an odd holiday, you know. Not exactly firecrackers and booze, more contemplative. We're supposed to apologize for wrongs we've done over the previous year, make right all our relationships. It's followed almost immediately by Yom Kippur, where we fast for a day to atone."

"Sound like good holidays to have." His voice was soft and sent a shiver up my spine.

I looked up, finding his gaze. "Do you think we could get together, just to talk?"

His mouth twitched. "Just talk? That's not something we've been good at in the past."

I nodded. "Maybe we could try again?"

Pete chewed his lower lip.

"Pete. I really am sorry. I'd do anything to change how things went down." I reached out. He stared at my hand resting on his arm.

A woman approached. I let go of him and stepped to the side so he could sell her two bunches of beets. With their deep green leaves and bright red roots, they looked more like a bouquet than a vegetable.

She paid, and Pete turned to me, folding his arms across his chest. "It's not just that. I can't do an open relationship. I'm not made that way."

Hope fluttered in my chest. "I'm not seeing anyone else."

He cocked his head to one side and watched me fidget for a few seconds. "We can talk. But no promises."

I glanced at the booth. "Where's Logan?"

Pete shook his head. "Football practice, of all things. Brynne's picking him up. I'm on my own." He checked his watch. When he looked up, a smile played at the edges of his eyes. "I assume that the fact you're here ten minutes before I close up means you were hoping we'd have this talk today?"

I straightened. "I'll help you load up."

"An injury-free Avi. That's a first." He bagged up my apples and honey.

I reached for my wallet and handed him a twenty. He started to shake his head, but I pressed it at him. "Take it. For once I'm employed."

He paused, took the money, and counted out my change. I set the bag down by my bike and started boxing up the apples while Pete sprinted off to retrieve the truck.

* * * *

The best place in town to drink outside is the Memorial Union Terrace. Pete found a metered spot next to the alumni house, and we walked through the golden afternoon light to the terrace. Across the upper patio, students slumped in the signature crayon-colored metal chairs, some reading thick textbooks, others in chatty groups. I bought a pitcher of stout at the takeout window and carried it down the steps to where Pete waited at one of the old wooden picnic tables next to the lake. I poured the beer, and for a few minutes we sat side by side, watching waves bounce the sailboats moored out in the lake. I'd been planning the conversation for days, but before it started and Pete turned me down again, I wanted to savor the feel of him beside me for a few more seconds.

In profile he looked like an old-time movie star. His hands splayed across his thighs were stained from handling beets. I took a deep breath and ran a finger along his pinky. He didn't pull away. I took it as a good sign. "I've spent too much time thinking about politics—historical and modern. It's made me cynical and stupid. Pete, I got it all wrong. I should have trusted you more."

He glanced at me. "And him less."

"Do you think you can forgive me?" I watched his hands.

He sighed. "I wish you'd believed in me to begin with."

"Me too." I looked up and met his eyes.

He held my gaze for a long time before whispering, "I forgive you." He looked out over the water. "I believe you're sorry. It sounds like you've had a rough couple of months. I'm no good at holding a grudge." He turned back to me with the beginnings of a smile. "Now Brynne, she might kill you."

While he was talking my heart started beating again. "Can we start over?"

He laughed dryly. "Do you know we were together less than two weeks?"

I nodded. "But you were right. It was something special."

Pete crooked his finger around mine and gazed at the lake. It was an eternity before he answered. "Letting you go hurt. Think how much worse it would be with more time together. I don't think I can do it. It might be better to leave things as they are."

I squeezed my eyes closed and took a deep breath and exhaled slowly. I wasn't going to cry. Not here. Not now.

"I'm rooted, Avi. I can't pick up and follow you wherever you go. You'll get a job in Oregon or New York, and I'll be broken again."

I wiped my eyes with my free hand, unwilling to let go of his finger. "I'm not going anywhere. Or at least I don't think I am. There's a job opening at the community college. I'm told I've got a good shot at it."

Pete's whole body turned toward me. "The community college here? In Madison?"

I searched his eyes for a response. "That's the plan."

He stared at me for a long moment. I held my breath.

A slow smile spread over his face. His hand entwined with mine. "You're staying."

I exhaled.

He cupped my jaw. "Do you think it would scandalize these young folk if I kissed you?"

"I don't give a fuck if it does."

He tasted sweeter than any new year deserved to be.

* * * *

When we got back to the farm, Brynne's arched eyebrows told me I had some apologizing to do there as well.

Pete grinned at his sister. "Where's Logan?"

"He's staying over at a friend's." Her gaze traveled down to our clasped hands and up again to my face.

Pete's smile broadened. "That's nice. Didn't you say you had errands to do this afternoon?"

She scowled. "Do you think this is a good idea? I mean, given how things worked out last time?"

I cleared my throat. "I know I was an asshole. I'm really sorry."

She considered me. "I'm not the one you should be apologizing to."

"Drop it," Pete whispered.

She looked at him. Their eyes locked in some sort of secret sibling communication. Eventually she shrugged. She turned to me. "If you hurt my brother again, I'll run you over with the thresher."

"Um, okay." Clearly she was going to take more of Ben Franklin's persistence than Pete had. In the meantime, it might be a good idea to steer clear of the heavy machinery.

She grabbed her bag, kissed Pete on the cheek, and strode out the door, calling, "I'll be back late. Don't wait up."

I watched the screen door bang shut. "Do you think I should go talk with her?"

"Later." Pete spun me toward him. I wrapped my arms around his waist as his hands gripped my shoulders. The kitchen clock ticked loudly. He pulled me into a kiss that tasted like beer and Pete. I fell into him like he was a desert oasis.

Pete ran his hands up my shoulders to cradle my face and deepened his kiss. I let my hands roam across his back, feeling the ropes of his muscles through the fabric of his shirt. I lost myself in the press of our bodies and the feel of his tongue twining with mine. Pete groaned into my mouth as I rubbed against him.

I broke the kiss long enough to say, "I want you."

"Bed," he murmured against my lips. "Now."

We raced up the steps, tossing off clothing as we went. I stumbled trying to kick off my shoe, and he laughed as he caught me. By the time we reached his room, we were naked, our clothes a lurid Hansel and Gretel trail.

I tackled him, and the bed jostled as we fell onto it. My body sang with the feel of his skin against mine. My leg slipped between his, and our bodies seemed to fuse. Pete arched into me, his cock a long tongue against my own. I tasted his golden skin and skimmed my hands across his thick shoulder muscles and down his strong chest. Pete's fingers sank into my ass cheeks as he pulled me against him in rhythm with his thrusts. My mouth found his, and we were kissing again, our tongues in a deep dance.

Pete rolled us over, and I was beneath him, his body a heavy caress.

I wrapped my legs around him, arching my ass up until our balls kissed as his cock slid against mine.

"I want you in me," I whispered and watched his eyes flare.

"Don't move." He stood and padded over to a chest of drawers. "I know I had some…. Wait…here." He held up a condom and a lube pillow.

"Seen much action lately?" I gestured to the cascade of socks he'd unearthed in the process of finding the supplies.

He shook his head and walked slowly toward the bed, his bouncing erection a riveting sight. "No. You?"

I held his gaze. "The last person in me was you."

He stopped. "Seriously?"

I rubbed my shoulder. "My last night with Jack didn't go very well. You might say things were over before they began."

He sat on the bed, his hand resting on my shoulder, his eyes dark. "What a prick."

I shrugged. "He was what he was."

Pete's gaze traveled down my body. "I'm glad you haven't been with anyone since we were together. It turns out I don't share well."

I slid my hand up his thigh and wrapped it around the silky length of his cock. "Imagine how I felt. There I was trying to be with him when I was falling in love with you."

He'd closed his eyes as I stroked his cock. They flew open. "Say that again."

"Imagine—"

Straddling me, he brought his face very close to mine. "Skip to the good part."

I looked up into his eyes, dark as the sky at dusk. "You mean the part about falling in love with you?"

A smile spread across his face. Those beautiful teeth gleamed down at me. "Yeah, I liked that part."

I patted the bedspread until my fingers touched the cool smoothness of the condom wrapper. I snagged it and brought it between us. Pete watched while I tore open the package and slipped out the latex disk. He pulled back and let me roll it on him. He looked away long enough to locate the lube pillow. His eyes stayed locked on mine as he emptied it onto his cock, using his hand to spread the slippery goo all over the rubber while he trailed the fingers of his other hand across my dick.

The world narrowed to the feel of his touch and the throb of my anticipation. A mirror on the far wall reflected the setting sun. The many shades of tan in Pete's skin were disappearing in the dimming light. A cow lowed in the pasture below, and Pete dropped down between my legs, his cock sliding down my balls to rest at the pucker of my ass. I pulled up my knees, holding them with my hands as I opened to him.

Pete looked down, watching himself as he pressed in. I closed my eyes and breathed, consciously relaxing around him. When I opened them again, he was focused on my face. I nodded, and he slipped in deeper. My breath quickened as the burn gave way to pleasure, and he buried himself in me all the way.

His gaze held mine as he fucked me, slowly at first, picking up speed. I looped my ankles over his shoulders and pushed against him as he thrust. The sound of him slapping against my ass sent a bolt of excitement through me so strong my cock leaked onto my stomach. He grasped and stroked it in rhythm with his hips. My heart beat in time with the pulse jumping in his neck. His breath came in rasps, or was that my own? I sensed his orgasm coming almost before I felt mine, a flutter deep in his eyes, the way his mouth tensed, the sweat in his hair. It seemed like sunlight spilled out of him, filling my body, my heart, igniting every inch of me until fire and heat were exploding out of both of us in a molten flow, filling the space between us, leaving us fused together, wet and hot and breathless.

I snuggled into his armpit and lobbed out the question I'd spent the last few days and nights hoping to ask. "Will you come home with me for Rosh Hashanah? There will be lots of painful silences and awkward glances. My sisters will mostly be okay, but my mom might be awful."

My head bounced with his laugh. "You make it sound tempting. How could I resist?"

"The thing is, you try to bring into Rosh Hashanah everything you want for the next year. I'd like to bring you."

He squeezed me to him. "Put it that way, of course I'll come."

"It really will be a sweet new year."

Pete pulled me closer and kissed the top of my head.

* * * *

I felt him stirring and glanced at the clock. We couldn't have been asleep more than an hour. "What's up?" I mumbled as he sat up.

He gazed down at me and brushed a lock of hair from my eyes. "Go back to sleep. I need to feed the animals and milk the cows."

I nodded and got up. "I'll help."

Pete raised an eyebrow but tossed me a pair of sweats.

Our footsteps rang in the empty house as we clomped downstairs. Pete reached for a sweatshirt hanging on a hook by the door and threw it to me. We stepped through the door into the cool autumn evening. I slipped on the bulky sweatshirt and rolled up the long sleeves as we crossed the yard toward the barn.

"You don't have to do this." Pete took my hand as we walked. "Although, if you're really wanting to atone, there's plenty of shit to shovel around here."

"If that's what it takes." I squeezed his hand. "I want to see if we can do this for real. I don't want us to be visitors in each other's lives."

He laughed. "I hope that doesn't mean I have to grade essays on American history, 'cause I'd much rather muck out barns."

As we neared the barn, I heard the cows shuffling and snorting. There was a strange sort of whining *baa* that Pete identified as the goats. Somewhere chickens chortled and a confused rooster crowed.

Pete let go of my hand and opened the barn door. I inhaled the smell of hay and manure and animals. He flipped a switch, and light cascaded down from bare bulbs, illuminating long rows of stalls.

I glanced around. "Where do you keep the pig? I'll feed it if you want."

Pete pulled me into his arms. "Gone. Logan got a good price for him at the fair. Next year we'll get Logan a calf. We're out of the pig-raising business."

I looked up into his brilliant smile. "I could learn to handle being a pig farmer. We are not our histories."

Pete shook his head. "You can stop trying so hard, Avi. I'm crazy about you too. Now come on. I'll teach you how to milk cows and goats."

I followed him through the warm barn and into what I hoped would be our fertile future.

The End

BONUS SHORT

Snakes and Ladders

One of my favorite things about September was the sweet smell of fallen apples. We did our best to harvest the fruit on time, but inevitably the wind knocked a few apples out of every tree, leaving the orchard fragrant with decaying fruit and buzzing with bees.

Avi probably should have been working on lectures or lesson plans or whatever it is that history professors did on Friday afternoons a few weeks into the fall term, but instead he had volunteered to help me pick apples to sell at the Saturday farmers' market. It was one of those perfect September days that make going back to school a cruel and unusual punishment. Avi's last class ended at three and by the time he got home, I was already ten feet off the ground with a bushel basket half full of gorgeous orange-red Pricilla apples. A few not so perfect specimens rattled around my shoulder bag, destined for our own cellars.

From my perch in the tree I watched him approach. Two years together and it still rocked my world to see him cross the field toward me. If anything, Avi was even better looking than when I first met him. He'd bulked out from working on the farm and the sun had deepened his olive skin to a rich golden brown. He'd lost that slump shouldered scholar look and walked across the field like a man who knew where he belonged. Right here. With me.

At the bottom of my ladder he smiled up at me. "Hey gorgeous, where do you want me to start?"

Where did I want him to start? Fuck the harvest, I wanted to roll around getting sweaty in the apple-scented grass. His smile widened like he knew exactly what I was thinking.

I glanced at the horizon, then up at the ridge top. It could wait. We had a little more than an hour of daylight left. With a sigh, I pointed the old MacIntosh tree. "The Ginger golds and Jonafrees won't be mature for another week, but the Mac needs picking."

"Got it." He collected a step ladder from under the Paula red tree we'd finished picking the week before and walked it over to the Mac.

Along with a few Honeycrisps and Cortlands, the MacIntosh had been one of a handful of trees my grandfather planted years ago. In his day, the apples fed the family and livestock. My father mainly ignored the trees. When my sister and I inherited the farm, one of the first things we did was to expand the orchard and add heirloom varieties that matured at different rates. It had taken a few years, but now we had a steady supply of apples to sell at the market from early August until the first deep freeze. Most of the orchard was now made up of spindly young trees like the one I was picking from and only a few gnarled grand dames like Avi's.

"Let me know if you find any storm damage." I called once he had settled the ladder under the most heavily laden branch. We'd had strong winds the night before. We didn't lose too many apples and the force wasn't bad enough to hurt the young trees, but the no matter how much we pruned the old guys, sometimes they couldn't take a punch. I watched Avi climb the ladder, wondering if I ought to switch with him. The last thing I wanted was for him to get hurt. Again. He wasn't exactly accident prone, but back when we were first together... As they say, shit happens.

"Don't look so worried, Pete." Avi called to me from his perch on the ladder. "I'm not the type to go out on a limb. Couldn't be safer." He plucked an apple and studied it with that mock serious look of his. "Of course, that's what Adam thought, isn't it?" He grinned at me and took a huge bite.

"Does that make me Eve?" I lobbed an ugly worm eaten apple at him.

He ducked. "Not Eve, Petey, you're my temptation."

Oh yeah. "Better get to picking them apples, Yeshiva boy. We need to fill a lot more bushels before I'll let you play with my snake."

I love to watch Avi laugh, love the way he throws back his head, abandoning his usual urbane countenance and committing to a moment of pure joy.

It took us almost an hour to fill the wooden crate boxes I had stacked on the ATV trailer, drive them back to the barn and load them into the truck. One more thing I wouldn't need to do before the sun came up. Avi slid the last of the crates to the front of the truck bed, leaving room for the fresh vegetables we'd pick and load at dawn. He climbed down and dusted off his jeans.

"I've got a surprise for you." At his raised eyebrows, I gestured toward the ATV, from which I'd unhitched the trailer. "Hop on."

I climbed on and he slid behind me.

He wrapped his arms around my waist and slid his hands lower. "Is this where I get to play with that snake?"

I leaned back into him, savoring his warmth and the excitement of his touch through my jeans. Reluctantly, I straightened. "Almost."

I started the ATV's engine. His hands moved from my crotch back to my waist but he stayed pressed close against my back. His breath tickled my neck, sending shivers down my spine. I gunned the engine, ready to get where we were going—fast.

We got to the top of the ridge in time to see the sun dip toward the horizon. The blanket was where I'd left it, spread out on the only high point of land we owned. From there we could see the entire farm, the orchard, vegetable fields, grazing cows, the barn and the old farmhouse.

"Wow." Avi whispered in my ear. "I feel like I just stepped into a Victorian novel—a buggy ride to a picnic in the early evening."

"Let's hope the squirrels didn't get into our cooler." I let him climb off first, then followed. No squirrel damage—the cooler still held bread, cheese and champagne. I popped open the champagne and poured us each a glass.

Avi was looking at me with an indulgent smile. "Will there be strolling minstrels passing by?"

Such a romantic. I sat on the blanket and smiled up at him. "Indulge me. We'll sit here and drink our champagne, watch the sunset, cuddle. It won't hurt, I promise."

He took the glass, sat and looked out at the sunset. "It's beautiful. Thanks."

I took a sip—cheap champagne, but it was the thought that counted. I leaned my head on Avi's shoulder. He put his arm around me. We watched silently as the sky lit with a blaze of color and the sun slid below the horizon.

"Dinner at your mom's house got me thinking." I drained the last of my glass, sat up and retrieved the bottle.

Avi sighed. "I know it's awkward. It was nice of you to come."

"It's getting easier. Give us all time to get used to each other." I refilled his glass and my own before going on. "It got me thinking about traditions—don't burst out into song, Tevya, that's not what I meant. I like the idea of family rituals and you know I love dipping apples in honey for a sweet new year. What I realized was that we've got you doing Christmas and Easter here at the farm with us, but ship the Jewish celebrations off to your mom's house. And while I'm happy to go there with you, I think we should develop some traditions of our own. How about an annual Rosh Hashanah picnic?"

"Sounds more like Succoth to me." Avi traced my jaw with his fingers.

Yet another holiday? "Succoth?"

He shook his head. "Doesn't matter. A Rosh Hashanah picnic with you sounds perfect to me."

His lips on mine were cool from the champagne but the kiss got hot quickly. When he pulled away it was dark, but even so I could see the shine of his eyes. He whispered, "God, I love you."

I set my glass down and wrapped my arms around him. "Wanna play with my snake?"

"Loose that mighty serpent. I promise not to bite."

An owl hooted in the woods nearby but I didn't care. He could watch if he wanted. I pulled Avi down beside me. It was going to be a very sweet new year.

Tarnished Souls 3:
Sacred Hearts

Dev Bentham

Chapter One

It was eight o'clock on an otherwise normal Sunday night. I'd just started table four's entrées when my phone buzzed.

"David Schwartz?" Whoever she was, she sounded young.

"What can I do for you?"

Her voice was gravelly. "Rick Miller's your business partner, right?"

"Yes." And more. My stomach clenched. What had he done now?

"I'm a dealer at Fortuna's. I shouldn't be calling you, but I think you should come get him."

I opened my mouth to speak, but the phone went dead.

He was gambling again. *Fuck.*

Sunday nights I cooked alone. The only other chef, the one who worked with me on weekends and covered two midday shifts, was busy throwing our money away. I stared at the food sizzling on my grill. Across the room, Billy rinsed and loaded a short stack of dishes. The door opened behind me, and young Fred stepped in, his tray piled with vinaigrette-stained salad plates.

I waved him over. "We're closing early. Lock the door, turn off the outside light, and tell Charmaine to close as soon as these guys are finished."

Billy looked up from the dishes. He wiped his stubbled face with the sleeve of his shirt. "What's up, boss?"

I shook my head. "Something I need to take care of." I looked at the half-cooked food, grilling prawns, a couple of salmon fillets, and a steak. Getting them plated would take me five minutes, max. How much damage could he do in five?

Charmaine arrived at my elbow as I garnished the last of the plates. "Why are we closing?"

I hung up my chef's coat. "Rick's at Fortuna's."

All the sweetness drained from her honey-brown skin. "I thought he quit."

Anger rolled around in my gut like a roulette wheel. I shook my head. "Evidently he started again."

She gave a curt nod and began stacking plates up her arm.

I bolted out the back door and sprinted toward my car.

Fortuna's Wheel Poker Palace was a squat orange stucco building in a neighborhood in far northeast Portland, a couple of miles from the restaurant. It took me twenty minutes to get there. People clustered around the doorway, smoking. I showed the doorman my ID and stepped inside. Groups of grim-faced people sat around felted tables, their arms resting on the padded table edge as they fingered various-sized stacks of brightly colored chips. It was surprisingly quiet for a room full of people. Sounds seemed to fall and die on the red, white, and black carpet. Someone laughed from across the room, where a handful of men leaned against the bar. I scanned the tables until I spotted his lucky straw cowboy hat.

As I got closer, I could see wisps of blond hair poking from beneath the brim. *Shit.* How long had he been sitting here losing our nest egg? I put a hand on his shoulder. Rick pushed his short stack of hundred-dollar black chips into the center of the table. *Shit.* Once they were out there, they couldn't be pulled back. The dealer, a young woman with raven hair, a rose tattoo on her shoulder, and sad eyes gave me one long glance before she dealt the cards. No one else at the table took cards. Tension shot through the stone-faced group, but I'd been here before with Rick. It didn't matter what the cards were. In the end he always lost. I hoped I could drag him away with something in his pocket. Our pocket. My father had been right. It was time to close the joint checking account. Again.

Rick had a three showing. He curled up the facedown card. An eight. He tapped the table. She tossed him an ace.

I closed my eyes. I heard Rick tap.

"Shit." It came out of him like breath.

I opened my eyes. The jack of hearts lay face-up next to the ace, three, and upturned eight. Twenty-two. The dealer raked in Rick's chips.

My grip closed around his shoulder. "Come on, let's go home."

He looked up at me. "Hey, just in time. You got some scratch I can use?"

I shook my head. "Not today."

He shrugged, pushed back from the table, and grinned at his fellow players. "Next time."

The dealer focused on her other customers and snapped open another deck.

* * * *

"What do you mean you emptied the business account?" I stared at Rick across our kitchen table. It was after midnight. I could smell the day's cooking fumes on my clothes, in my hair. Rick looked handsome, contrite, and ready to be forgiven. Again.

He stared at the coffee cup he was passing back and forth between his hands. "I was so close. If I'd had a few more chips, I could have turned it around."

"You promised you would never gamble again. 'Not even a lottery ticket.' That's what you said when you begged me to trust you."

"I know." He leaned forward, his eyes ablaze. "But this is it, Davey. I can feel it, like fire in my veins. My luck is right here."

"Clearly." I glared at him until he looked away. "How are we going to make payroll or pay the vendors? That money wasn't yours to throw away."

His gaze flicked to mine. His voice rose and fell like that of a thwarted two-year-old. "But if I win, we can get that new stove you want. Maybe take a vacation. I'm doing this for us."

The chair clattered to the floor as I stood. "That's bullshit. You didn't gut our business for us. And since when did you care about us having a vacation? Remember the Caribbean cruise we had to cancel because you gambled away our vacation fund? Christ, Rick, it's taken us three years to build up a safety cushion for the restaurant, and now we're back at square one. We'll need to stretch our credit to the limit to pay this month's bills."

He shifted in his chair.

"Tell me."

He cleared his throat. "Yeah, about that. I meant to tell you, but I thought I'd get it back right away."

I opened my mouth, closed it. My voice came out in a whisper. "The business equity loan?"

He nodded, his eyes fixed on the table.

"Our credit cards?"

He looked up at me from under those thick eyelashes I used to love.

My throat was closing up. I downed what was left of my orange juice before croaking out, "Do we have anything left?"

He pursed his lips, drummed his fingers, tapped his feet, shuffled his butt, and eventually shook his head. "But I'm gonna get it back. Plus a lot more. I tell you, my luck's — "

"Fuck your luck." I grabbed the table edge to keep myself from falling as my carefully constructed world fell apart.

The image of those four dinners I'd finished plating after the dealer called me floated into my head. What had they cost me? I pictured the stack of black chips. A hundred dollars each. Five minutes. Maybe three hands of blackjack. What did that add up to? My car payment? A week's payroll? If I'd let those dinners go, what would I have been able to keep?

I forced him to meet my gaze. His deep blue eyes had that pleading look that always got me. But not this time. I felt nothing but contempt for both of us. Whatever self-destructive part of me that kept drawing me back to Rick seemed as drained as our bank accounts. When I could speak again, I whispered, "Go. We're done. Leave the keys to the apartment, to the restaurant, and get out of here. I don't want to see you again."

I could see the beginnings of his protest. Something in my look stopped him. He stood and walked to the bedroom. I leaned against the table, listening to him pack. It didn't matter what he took with him. There wasn't anything worth having that he hadn't already stolen.

* * * *

I woke with my heart pounding. In my dream, I'd been running from something big and terrifying. What it had been faded as I opened my eyes to take in the familiar walls of my bedroom, gray in the dim dawn light. There'd been something else. Not scary but beautiful. A man emerging from the waves. Light streamed from somewhere behind him, and I couldn't make out the details of his face, only that he was tall. Tall and thin with a halo of wild curls.

My pulse slowed, fear dissolving into sadness as I registered the open empty drawers and the gaping space in the closet where Rick's clothes used to hang. It was a bittersweet relief to have him gone. After all, I'd been lonely for a long time. I pictured the man from my dream holding out his arms. That's what I wanted — something deep, sweet, and real. *Right*. Now I was planning happiness with an imaginary lover.

I threw off the covers and sat on the edge of the bed. This wasn't the time to wallow in regrets or fantasies. I needed to face up to the wreckage I'd allowed Rick to make in my life and start picking up the pieces. The only thing to do was get up, make myself some coffee, and take a dose of reality.

There's a mind-numbing, free-fall feeling when every account is empty, every line of credit maxed.

After checking all our accounts online and confirming that we were beyond broke, I closed every last one of them. The last thing I needed was for Rick to figure out a way to get us further into debt. I called the lawyer Papa recommended. As a favor to my father, he agreed to squeeze me in before lunch.

* * * *

The restaurant was dark and smelled of seared meat and floor cleaner. I jotted the janitor's name on my list of people I needed to call so I could explain that no one was getting paid because I'd believed in my asshole boyfriend's so-called recovery. I should have known better than to trust him. Again. What's a relationship without trust? That thought was the sucker button in the middle of my chest that Rick knew how to push every time. I stood in the middle of my slaughtered little restaurant, my stomach clenching with anger. Damned if I'd trust him ever again.

It could have been worse. When we'd opened the restaurant, Rick had argued we should go big, with a huge, noisy kitchen full of chefs cranking out entrées by the dozen and an elegant dining room that could seat a hundred. I thought we should start small and eclectic. A few tables and a limited menu, open only for dinner. Done right, the place would seem exclusive, I'd said. And it was all we could afford. Since I'd had the good credit and written the business plan, I'd won.

Now I looked around at the dark blue walls covered in local art. I'd need to contact the artists so they could take their work home. I ran my hand along the back of one of the ancient chairs we'd bought at auction and spent long hours refinishing in the months before the restaurant opened. Covered with bright floral linens that always reminded me of Mexico, my ten tables sat ready for dinner. I straightened a crooked knife at one setting. Crisp white napkins folded like lilies marked each place. The sight usually made me smile as I imagined the beautiful plates of food to come. This morning it had me eyeing a bottle of good brandy beside the wine rack.

The cash register opened with a sigh. I thumbed the ones, fives, tens, and twenties. I knelt to open the safe. Sunday nights are slow, and we'd closed early, so I wasn't surprised that the blue deposit bag felt slimmer than usual. I pulled out the deposit slip, written in Charmaine's careful script. About six hundred. With the drawer, that meant I had less than a thousand dollars, which wouldn't make a dent in what I owed. Credit card receipts would be sucked into my void of debt, but there was some currency and a few checks I could cash. Reaching into the back of the safe, I retrieved the pink plastic box Rick had bought to hold spare rolls of quarters, dimes, nickels, and pennies. He'd drawn eyes and a snout on it and called it our piggy bank. Inside was thirty-seven dollars and fifty cents. I added the rolls of coins to my pile of cash and checks and stared at the box, which he'd presented to me with great ceremony on our opening night. I had a sudden urge to break the fucking thing, see it splinter under my heel. Instead I tossed it into the trash and gathered my paltry stack of money.

I left the drawer alone, slid the deposit into my jacket pocket, and started dialing phone numbers, calling in the troops for what promised to be the worst staff meeting ever. I got through to most and left messages for the rest. I went to the kitchen to continue my dismal inventory.

* * * *

Abraham Klein had an office on the fifth floor of an ornate building in the historic district. It was furnished simply, with gleaming pine floors and upholstered wooden chairs. The view consisted of other old buildings, seen through ancient, double-hung windows. His secretary, a tall, thin woman with gray hair swept into a bun, waved me through. Abe stood to shake my hand with the same firmness and warmth as the last time I saw him, during the High Holidays—the only time I ever made it to Temple.

He gestured for me to sit. "Your father said something about money trouble?"

I nodded and cleared my throat, humiliation blooming in my gut. "My partner has a gambling problem."

Abe's brow wrinkled. "Business partner?"

I looked down at my white knuckles. "That too."

His chair creaked. When I looked up, he was peering from over tented fingers. "Does he… It is he?"

I nodded.

"Does he have access to your assets?"

I snorted. "He did. When I had assets."

"Ah. Show me."

I spread my papers out across his desk. After a few minutes, he looked up again. "I take it you've closed these accounts?"

I shrugged. "Too little, too late, but yes."

"And Mr. Miller" — he looked from the bank statements to my loan account balances — "why isn't he a co-borrower on these loans?"

It felt like a bottomless pit of shame was opening in my belly. "He, um, he wasn't a good enough credit risk."

Abe stared at me for a long moment. "What is the status of your relationship now?"

My head hurt. I rubbed at my temples. "It's over."

"Good." His sharp eyes were surprisingly kind. "Your options are limited, and I'm afraid the burden of debt falls directly on you."

I sighed.

He leaned back in his chair and contemplated me with a fatherly look. "If it helps, in my experience, people are only betrayed by the ones they're closest to."

I shook my head. "That's hardly comforting. Where do I go from here?"

* * * *

The first place I went after meeting Abe was to an AA meeting. People nodded to me in greeting, and someone offered me a cup of coffee. In the ten years I'd been frequenting church basements, I'd been to good meetings and bad meetings and meetings that rocked my world, but I'd always walked out feeling better than I did when I sat down.

This was no exception. A guy with thirty days talked about facing jail time for a DUI, and I realized that closing a restaurant wasn't the worst thing in the world. An old-timer reminded us all to be grateful for what was working and to turn the rest over to our Higher Power. I took a deep breath and thought about that. I was healthy and still relatively young. Whatever the devastation Rick had wreaked in my life, it wouldn't last forever. By the time the meeting ended and I caught a bus back to the restaurant, I was determined to make it through this one long, hard, fucking sucky day, even if it took going one hour at a time.

We opened at six, so I scheduled the staff meeting for four. How long could it take to tell eight people they were out of a job?

Charmaine arrived first. It was her night off, so she had the baby asleep in a sling across her chest. I was sitting at the table nearest the kitchen, filling out the first few pages of my bankruptcy paperwork.

She settled into a chair across from me. "This isn't good, is it?"

I shook my head. "He wiped us out. We're going under."

She closed her eyes. "When?"

I looked down at my inventory list. "Soon.

We've enough food for a few days, maybe a week with some creative menu manipulation. But there's nothing for wages."

"Nothing?"

The door opened. Billy and Fred came in, trailed by the rest of the kitchen and waitstaff. They were laughing and talking until they spotted Charmaine and me sitting in depressed silence at the back of the room. The group formed a tight circle around us. They waited for me to speak.

Rigorous honesty. It was one of the first principles I'd learned in treatment. I'd been trying to practice it in all my affairs for ten years. Sometimes it was easier than others. I looked at their faces. Charmaine with her new baby. Billy, coming out of his own stint in rehab. Fred, whose mother had leukemia. People who depended on income from my restaurant to pay their rent, feed their families, and repay student loans.

I told them what I'd told Charmaine, that we were flat broke. Fred stared at me open-mouthed. Billy jammed his hands into his pockets and seemed to shrink into himself. Watching them, I felt a leaden mixture of guilt and sadness that made it hard to continue.

With an effort I took out the deposit envelope from the night before and pulled out eight small bundles of bills, each held by a paper clip. I handed one to each of them. "This is all I could salvage from last night's receipts. There's forty-seven dollars for each of you. It's all I've got. I'll start making calls tomorrow, see if anyone's hiring. I'm planning on staying open until the food runs out. If any of you are up for that, we can split the till each night until it stops making sense. If you're not interested, don't worry about it. Everyone's getting my highest recommendation. You've been a wonderful crew."

When I was done, there was silence. Charmaine wiped away a tear. A couple of the others started shrugging on coats. I pulled two bottles of wine from the shelf behind me. "I've got some work to do in back. You guys have a drink on me. For anyone who wants to stay and work, we'll open in an hour."

I went back to the kitchen and turned on some music. I didn't want to hear them deciding what to do.

After a while, Charmaine joined me.

"How's it look out there?"

Charmaine shrugged. "Most everyone's gone home to polish their résumés. Billy's helping Fred set up." She gestured toward the baby. "I can't afford to get a sitter, but I can go home and pick up her playpen if you like. Billy said she'd be fine in the corner by him."

"You don't have to do that." I stroked the soft hair on the baby's head.

She shrugged. "I was here your first night. Might as well be here your last." She gazed at me for a long moment, hand on her hip. "You know you deserve better than Rick, right? Give it time, honey, and the right man will come along." She turned and strode out the door.

I stared after her. The right man? After putting up with Rick for so long, I deserved a fucking saint. Except it was my own damned fault. I was the one who kept taking him back.

It was quarter to six when Charmaine returned, a folded playpen beneath her arm and an overstuffed baby bag over her shoulder. Billy babbled at the baby from his sink full of prep pans, and it occurred to me that he probably had grandchildren somewhere, left behind in his gutter-drunk days. Charmaine handed the squirming bundle to him while she set up the playpen in the corner, safe from the hot dishwasher spray. Billy gurgled up at the baby, who pumped her fists in the air in reply.

As Charmaine started out the kitchen door, I called, "Don't take credit cards. Checks and cash only, otherwise we'll never see the money."

She gave a curt nod and went to open the door.

* * * *

Word got around by the second night, and we were slammed. People kept coming back into the kitchen to say how sorry they were to see us close. By the next night we had to reduce the menu offering substantially, and by Wednesday it was clear we had to close. After closing Wednesday night, I cooked us all the best dinner I could scavenge. I emptied the cash register, dividing everything we had into four neat piles. I sent the rest of the wine home with Charmaine and Fred, gave Billy my supply of soft drinks, and emptied the walk-in and the pantry into grocery bags for all three of them. I took one last look at my beautiful, airy restaurant before locking the doors and driving home.

I spent two days wheedling and found part-time jobs for everyone on staff, although no one needed a chef. After that, it took two weeks and a giant garage sale to sell it all—the restaurant equipment, apartment furniture, sound system, my car. My life shriveled, until everything I owned fit into my two bags. The proceeds paid a week's severance for the staff and the flat fee for Abe Klein. I defaulted on debts to vendors, broke two leases—one on the apartment, one on the restaurant—all of which pretty much guaranteed I wouldn't be opening another place anytime soon. Good thing Portland had an excellent public transportation system, since I was about to be job hunting in a saturated market. Two years of cooking school, ten years of experience, three years running my own trendy place, and I'd be lucky to find a job as a greasy diner short-order cook.

Available now from Loose-id

Look for Sacred Hearts from

Love is a Light Press December 2014

Dev Bentham

Dev Bentham writes soulful m/m romance. Her characters are flawed and damaged adult men who may not even know what they are missing, but whose lives are transformed by true love.

Love is a Light Titles by Dev Bentham

August Ice

* * * *

The TARNISHED SOULS Series
Learning from Isaac
Fields of Gold

Coming soon to Love is a Light:
Sacred Hearts
Bread, Salt and Wine

Other books by Dev
Driving into the Sun
Nobody's Home
Painting in the Rain
Moving in Rhythm

www.ingramcontent.com/pod-product-compliance
Lightning Source LLC
Chambersburg PA
CBHW060150130626
46556CB00006B/2573